A BOY
CALLED
HPE

Sometimes a little bit of hope
can go a long way

A BOY CALLED HOPE

LARA WILLIAMSON

USBORNE

First published in the UK in 2014 by Usborne Publishing Ltd., Usborne House, 83-85 Saffron Hill, London EC1N 8RT, England. www.usborne.com

Photography: World, page 9, 71, 187, 221, 274 © leonello calvetti/Shutterstock; TV, page 24, 209 © Ensuper/Shutterstock; Virgin Mary, page 83 © doraclub/ Shutterstock; Shrimp, page 174 © Alexander Raths/Shutterstock

A CIP catalogue record for this book is available from the British Library.

ISBN 9781409570318   JFMAMJJA OND/14   03192/07

Printed in Chatham, Kent, UK.

To Millie, with all my love.

For you I'd travel 238, 857 miles to the moon.

CHAPTER 1

I'm Dan Hope, and deep inside my head I keep a list of things I want to come true. For example: I want my sister, Ninja Grace, to go to university at the North Pole and only come back once a year for twenty-four hours. I want to help Sherlock Holmes solve his most daring mystery yet. And if it could be a zombie mystery, all the more exciting. I want to be the first eleven-year-old to land on the moon. When I get there I want to say, "One small step for boy, one giant headache for his mother." I want my dog to stop eating planets and throwing them up on the carpet. And finally, the biggest dream of all,

I want my dad to love me.

The last one is the most difficult to achieve, even harder than persuading my mum to let me travel approximately 238,857 miles to the moon. To be honest, I'd been getting along without him. Not that it was easy living without a dad, but I'd managed to keep my feelings squashed inside, until today. Today, everything changes.

I'm on the sofa eating a peanut butter sandwich when it happens. Dad appears on my TV screen, right under my nose, right in my living room, where he hasn't been for years. At first the sandwich attaches itself to the roof of my mouth. That's what I love about peanut butter. It's so sticky it's a wonder they don't put it in tubes and sell it as glue. I have to do tongue gymnastics to stop myself choking. Already this isn't turning out like a normal Monday evening in Paradise.

If I could, I would switch Dad off. Flick the button, say goodbye, let him dissolve into blackness. But there's something wrong about making your dad invisible without asking his permission. As if he can read my thoughts, Dad looks up at me, holds my gaze and nods. To say this is a surprise is an understatement. I don't mind admitting my shock soon changes into something else, a sort of stunned delight at seeing Dad back at 10 Paradise Parade where he belongs. Okay, so there is the small matter of him being a TV presenter and there being a glass screen between us that wasn't there before. But it's still so amazing that I smile. It is, I believe with all certainty, the smile of a boy whose dad is back in his life. Actually, it's the smile of a boy whose teeth are glued together with peanut butter.

When Ninja Grace wanders into the living room and glances at the TV screen, her mouth assumes a stunned-goldfish position. "Dad", she bubbles, "is on our TV."

Someone give my sixteen-year-old sister a medal.

"What kind of fresh hell is this?" Ninja Grace says. "There should be an eleventh commandment for dads: Thou shalt not walk out on your family and then turn up four years later in a glamorous TV job. This is all kinds of wrong."

How can it be wrong? I blink back my confusion. Even Moses would be happy that Dad is back in our lives. Surely it's epic. All right, it's not exactly how we imagined welcoming him home. No fairy cakes, the rainbow-coloured hundreds and thousands bleeding into vanilla frosting, and no writing his name out in sparklers. But he's still under our noses and we can see him every day. Must-watch TV, that's what it is. Ninja Grace is out of her tiny mind if she doesn't realize how brilliant this could be for us.

In fact, this is the best thing that's happened to me since Mum bought me a mossy-green skateboard with high-performance bearings.

"Not pleased to see him then?" I ask.

A string of saliva stretches inside Ninja Grace's mouth. "One taxi straight to the nuthouse for Daniel Hope, if he thinks our dad being on TV is a good thing," she says. The string snaps.

Ninja Grace wasn't always Ninja Grace, by the way. Once upon a time she was as normal as a sister could be. But all that changed when she turned thirteen. That's when she turned into a *word ninja*. By the way, a word ninja is someone who uses words as a weapon. Whatever you say, the word ninja will  hit back at you with their insult arrows. Think you're smart? Think again, because a word ninja will wound you instantly with their cutting remarks. That is exactly what Grace Hope turned into when she became a teenager, and that is exactly why Ninja Grace is screaming at me now.

"That man is dead to this family."

Word ninja fires a dagger at my back!

"And you'd better accept it if you know what's good for you."

Ninja Grace is shooting from the lip.

But whatever the ninja says, this time it will not be enough to stop me thinking that this is brilliant. If Dad has been catapulted to fame, then his children will be famous too. The kids at school will beg for my autograph. From this day forward I'll be a star at Our Lady of the Portal School. I can see it all now: I'll have my own web page. I'll go super viral. Perhaps I'll have my own newspaper. *The Son*, I'll call it. The boys will ask me to be the captain of the football team and the girls will write *Mrs Dan Hope* in their notebooks. What's more, the dinner ladies will put extra helpings of chips 'n' curry on my plate and I'll say I couldn't possibly eat that much and they'll say I can because they love watching my famous dad on TV. (I think this is what Mum calls "to curry favour".)

To be honest, Dad always wanted to be on the telly so I guess it shouldn't have been that much of a surprise. Interviewing, dealing with the public and talking – he was good at the lot. Mind you, we didn't think he'd ever leave his job as a journalist on the local newspaper. How wrong we were. Fast-forward four years, job and children left behind and – wham – hello, star TV man.

It's the leaving-your-children-behind bit that hurts the most. I was only seven when Dad walked out. The day started like any other but ended up with me sitting at the top of the stairs with Grace. She was twelve and still normal in those days. Drawers were banging in the kitchen and I remember thinking Mum must be angry. I didn't want to eat the dinner she was cooking if she was so mad about it. It had to be cottage pie. Cottage pie always made me angry too because the mince was full of rubbery bits that bounced off my teeth. Grace said the correct name for the rubbery bits was gristle. There was this *doof-doof* sound and a noise like someone whistling through a blade of grass. Grace looked at me and said she didn't really think this was about cottages or gristle. Dad was trying to calm Mum down but really he was cranking her up. Over and over again, Mum said she was very upset about The Other Woman.

In the end I thought they were talking a foreign language because Grace said, "It's all Greek to me." And my bum was so numb that I knew if I didn't move I'd never be able to straighten up or walk like I wasn't a baboon. But Grace said I couldn't leave, as it was getting exciting because Dad was talking about going on a whole new adventure while Mum was shouting about playing around. Grace said this was great news because it would mean fun for us all.

Maybe we'd be going on a family holiday. Only then Dad was shouting about being on his own and I wasn't sure that it sounded like the sort of laugh-a-minute holiday I wanted. Not once did he mention caravans or candyfloss. Or even us.

I didn't hear what Dad said next because his voice was flat and there was a thump that sounded like a big ham dropping on the kitchen table. Mum was crying and the drone of it went up and down as if she was single-handedly flying a light aircraft. Mum shouted that she was sick of his extra-curricular activities and Dad said he couldn't take it any more and he'd had enough of her histrionics. (When I pressed her on the matter, Grace whispered that histrionics was a subject at school.)

At that moment the kitchen door flew open and Grace slithered snake-style on her belly towards her bedroom so she wasn't spotted by Dad. But me, I couldn't move. Dad opened the front door and let it slam behind him. The daffodils on the wallpaper vibrated with the force.

I returned to my bedroom, glad the whole thing was over. I vowed I'd never eat a cottage pie, speak a foreign language, study histrionics or walk like a baboon. (Well, maybe I'd walk like a baboon because that could be kind of funny.) But after that evening, things went a bit weird.

We weren't allowed to get chips from the local chip shop, The Frying Squad, any more. According to Grace, who had sussed out the whole thing, Dad had run off with the woman who worked there. Busty Babs was her name and Grace said luring men in with fried spuds was her game. Grace said Dad had "had his chips" and that was that. I argued that I'd had my chips from there too. Grace said my chips weren't his chips and Dad wasn't coming back. In fact, he was gone for ever. I shrugged, because at seven years old I thought for ever would last a week or a month.

How wrong I was.

For ever did mean for ever.

On the outside I might look like any other eleven-year-old boy. But on the inside, I'm full of bright ideas. At Our Lady of the Portal School they do not recognize this amazing ability I have, which is a shame. Then again, I hide it well because that way I can continue thinking my bright ideas while my teacher, Mrs Parfitt, is boring everyone with maths. On this very day, the day after seeing Dad on the telly, and while Mrs Parfitt is attempting to get into the *Guinness World Records* for the largest amount of waffling one human being can do on the subject of BODMAS, I am finalizing a cunning plan. Seeing Dad on the TV was incredible but now I want more. While Mrs Parfitt babbles on about brackets, orders, division, multiplication, addition and subtraction, I think about how much I want Dad to talk to me and how I'm going to make it happen.

"Pssst," whispers Jo Bister. "I've got a new saint relic in my collection. It's the best one ever. You've got to see it to believe it."

I shrug. "I thought the deal with saints is you don't have to see them to believe them."

Jo mumbles that I think I'm so clever. Which, technically, I am. "This bit of fabric," she says, keeping an eye on Mrs Parfitt, "swiped the feet of someone who touched the feet of someone else who kissed the feet on the statue of Saint Christina the Astonishing."

You cannot give an answer back to a person who thinks they have a hotline to God. You may try but you will fail. What you will do is go along with them and pretend you are as loopy as they are. This method has worked for me for many years. Ever since reception, Jo Bister and I have been friends. In those days she was interested in finger-painting the walls with snot and I was into grabbing her plaited hair and shouting "Gee-up", pretending she was a show pony. I sort of wish she was still digging out bogeys instead of all this religious stuff. She says these relics help her to be a better person. In fact, she even brushes her teeth in holy water because she says it means every word that escapes her lips will be a kind one.

By the way, that's total rubbish. Yesterday, she said I had a spot that resembled Mount Vesuvius. Holy water didn't make her say that. I might add that Jo still has freakishly long hair, despite me tugging on it when we were five. She says she won't ever cut it because there is a lot of superpower in hair, just ask Samson. (Our neighbour has a dog called Samson, but I don't think she's talking about him because his only superpower is yapping.)

My second friend at Our Lady of the Portal is Christopher. He's new to the area and only joined the school at the beginning of September. When he arrived, the teacher asked him where he came from and he laughed and said the Emerald Isle. Mrs Parfitt's eyes looked like someone had lit a match behind them, and she set a globe of the world on her desk before telling the class that the Emerald Isle was the third largest island in Europe and approximately 6.3 million people lived there. She called Christopher up to the front of the classroom and asked him to point out the Emerald Isle. Christopher said he didn't think the Emerald Isle was on this globe because it was just the nickname for the Ireland housing estate, ten minutes' walk from school.

At break I sidled up to Christopher, shook his hand and told him I welcomed anyone to the school who could make Mrs Parfitt go the colour of the skin under a picked scab. Christopher looked at me as if I was a two-headed alien and walked away. That was the beginning of our friendship though, and a few days later, when Jo was telling me about her plastic glow-in-the-dark statue of Our Lady of Knock, Christopher came over and said he enjoyed playing guitar. He was also a green belt in tae kwon do and had a hamster. When Jo asked the hamster's name, Christopher shouted, "Boo!" and Jo said a word that was anything but saintly and nearly fell backwards over the wall. Apparently, Boo was the hamster's name. Jo admitted that Saint Francis of Assisi would have loved the hamster, even if it had a stupid name. And I told her to shut up because the name Boo was far more astonishing than the name Saint Christina the Astonishing. Christopher said he wanted to know more about Jo's saints and asked her to go through the alphabet, naming a saint for every letter.

Jo thought about it for a moment and replied, "Is this a holy wind-up?"

The following day, like the prodigal father, Dad returns to the TV. "Hey, Dad," I announce. "I'm going to get in contact with you." But Dad acts as if he can't hear me so I pretend I am him, talking to me.

"Are you?" says Dad. I make my voice as deep as possible.

"Oh yes," I reply. "I've got this bright idea. You'll be impressed. In fact" – I lean towards the TV screen until my breath steams his face – "you'll want to get to know me all over again."

Dad pushes up his glasses then shuffles some papers on his desk. "Sounds exciting, Dan. When is it going to happen?"

I change my voice once more. "Don't be too impatient. Mum says good things come to those who wait." Then I say, "But it won't be long." I pick up a toy pirate that's sitting on the coffee table. "Before you know it we'll be sailing into an adventure together."

The living room door opens and Ninja Grace appears. "Are you talking to yourself?" She grunts as I put the pirate on top of a magazine.

"He's going to the island of um...Glamour," I say, "on the good ship *Fancy Celebrity Who I Don't Know The Name Of*."

"You're about to sail on the good ship *Psychiatrist*," Ninja Grace spits. When she turns towards the TV screen she makes a vacuum of her mouth, sucking all the air out of the room. "Watching Dad again? Quit torturing yourself. And before you get any ideas about telling people your dad is a celeb, don't bother. You wouldn't want them to think we're so boring he abandoned us for a better life."

I shrug. "He did, didn't he?"

"Oh yeah, but we don't need to broadcast the fact. You might be okay being labelled boring, but I don't want it. I told Mum he's on the telly and she says we should keep it to ourselves and get on with our own lives. We don't need his kind of fame and fortune, nor do we need to live in a big house."

I hadn't thought of that. Dad's house will be massive, like Buckingham Palace x 3, with hundreds of windows and a Union Jack stuttering in the wind. The flag will have his initials on it: MM, like the Queen is ER. Surrounding the house will be a huge wall with electronic gates, two roaring lions will guard the front door and there will be a lawn so heavily clipped it's like it's had a number two haircut. I'll have my own room in the Malcolm Maynard mansion and it will be the size of a football pitch and I'll be allowed to paint my walls purple because that's the colour of kings. Perhaps Dad will have a snappy little dog to warn off intruders. It could be like Samson, Mrs Nunkoo's dog from number three. Samson looks like a cross between a shih-tzu and a poodle. I call it a shihtz-poo. Thinking about it, I'm not sure Dad would want one of those.

"Put Dad out of your head," says Grace, eyeballing me.

I pick up the pirate again. "I have no plans whatsoever," I say, manoeuvring the pirate to the edge of the coffee table. "If I had any thoughts of going on a quest, I have squashed them like a doubloon trampled under the foot of a one-eyed, overweight pirate with a parrot squawking, 'Pieces

of eight!' in his ear. Nope, I would rather walk the plank than search for the treasure I desire."

"You're weird," replies Ninja Grace, prising the pirate from my fingers and throwing it onto the floor.

"Awww...you've thrown him into the Ocean of Swirly Carpet."

That evening, as I lie on the bed playing my guitar,

thoughts of Dad gallop through my mind. I've missed him. As my fingers find the strings, I think about how I need a dad in my life. It's as if, all those years ago, I planted a little Dad seed in my soul. I watered it and cared for it and suddenly, without me realizing, it has turned into a leafy tree. I hum softly. Mum would flip if she knew I was making plans to contact Dad, but that's because she's loved-up with the new boyfriend she met in June. Big Dave, he's called. He owns Kwik Kars and apparently their eyes met over the bonnet of our old Charade. The Charade has gone now but they've been together for six months. Music puddles into the dark corners of my bedroom and I play until my fingers ache and I have to stop.

"Dad," I whisper into the darkness.

"Yes, Dan," I reply in my gruffest voice.

"You still want me in your life, don't you? I mean, you wouldn't hurt me a second time, would you?"

Dad doesn't answer.

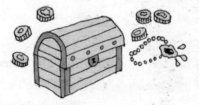

CHAPTER 2

From: Dan Hope
<dansherlockhope@deemail.com>
Sent: 22 November 07:54
To: Malcolm Maynard
<malcolmjmaynard@silverdreamstv.com>
Subject: HELLO

Hi Dad,
When I first saw you on telly I was more surprised than when Charles Scallybones the First (the dog Mum bought me when you left) threw up in my school trainers and I put my feet in them. I thought,

there is my Dad and he's FAMOUS. As you can see, I'm so excited it deserves caps.

I have tried to imagine what it will be like when you reply to this email, but I can't. So if you'll reply then I won't have to.

By the way, Grace is still alive. She has this new boyfriend called Stan, but enough of her.

Back to me: I am eleven now, I can play the guitar, and I'm an expert on a skateboard and the mysteries of Sherlock Holmes. Bet you'd forgotten that you left two books on our bookshelf. One was about getting to the bottom of piles and the other was a book about Sherlock Holmes and how he solved all these mysteries. Well, guess what. I tried to read the one on piles but there were too many strange illustrations, so I read the one on Sherlock Holmes instead. Twice.

I've also redecorated my bedroom since you last saw it. My bed looks like it has been dumped in a galaxy. Imagine lots of glow-in-the-dark stars tacked to the ceiling and you'd be right. And I've got a hanging planet mobile that Big Dave, Mum's friend, bought me. Grace isn't all that impressed with it. She says no one wants to look up at Uranus. And Mum moans about the mess on the bedroom floor and says my room's a black hole. I looked up black holes and they're a region in space where nothing can escape, not even light. There are different black hole classifications. A supermassive black hole is $\sim10^5$–10^{10} M_{Sun}. An intermediate black hole is $\sim10^3 M_{Sun}$. A stellar black hole is $\sim10 M_{Sun}$ and a micro black hole is up to $\sim M_{Moon}$. When I told Mum about this she said the black hole in my bedroom is supermassive.

I've never been described as supermassive before. I could get used to this.

That's all my news. Could you send me an email telling me what you've been up to? It would be nice if we could be pen pals. Do you think we could meet up soon? You don't have to come to 10 Paradise Parade. I could come to your palace instead. That would be even better than the supermassive black hole.

Please reply to my email address as soon as possible. I got yours from the TV website. Clever, aren't I? Mum says I take after her, although I'm not sure this is strictly true.

Love, Dan. :)

As I walk down Paradise Parade towards school, I feel different. I probably look different. It's as though I'm surrounded by a mist of golden ectoplasm. One that says: *Dan Hope is the happiest boy in the universe because he has contacted his dad.* I even wave and shout, "Hello!" to Mrs Nunkoo as she nudges Samson into the garden. He cocks his leg and releases a golden arch onto her slippers. Mrs Nunkoo waves back but looks mildly surprised. I'd like to think this is because she's spotted my magical glow but I think it's because her feet are steaming.

Turning into Agapanthus Road, I allow myself a little smile. In my mind, I can see Dad opening his emails. His mouth makes an O of surprise when he realizes that his long-lost son has got in touch. Perhaps he's so happy he's wiping away a tiny teardrop. No, no, that's too much, but Dad can't wait to send me an email back. That message will say that he's sorry for walking out and not being part of my life. The email will be waiting for me when I get home from school.

It isn't.

The ectoplasm might have lost a bit of its glow but I'm not going to let myself feel too sad. After all, Dad's a busy man now he's on TV. He's probably signing autographs and attending village fêtes and turning up to the opening of an envelope. That's what Mum says celebrities do these days. I bet I'll hear from him later this evening, or even tomorrow morning before I go to school.

I don't.

★ ★ ★

The following day when I walk towards school, the golden ectoplasm has been replaced by a stodgy black cloud. Mrs Nunkoo is bringing in the milk and shouts, "Hello!" and I mumble back as though I have a mouth full of scrambled eggs. My eyes don't move from the pavement as I turn into Agapanthus Road. It seems my cunning plan hasn't gone according to plan. Why hasn't Dad answered yet? The question is on a merry-go-round inside my head.

Last night, when Mum was doing the evening shift at Aladdin's Supermarket and Grace was at Stan's, I switched on the TV and Dad popped up. I watched him for any signs that he'd read my email. I wasn't expecting him to be wearing a big badge, but I was hoping I'd see *something*. Perhaps there would be a twitch or a tugging of his earlobe, a secret message between father and son. There was nothing. Dad looked completely calm. In fact, I'd almost say Dad hadn't given me any thought at all. And I was so annoyed that I didn't bother having a conversation with him because I knew I'd end up arguing with myself.

"What's up with you?" asks Jo, in between drinking from the water fountain in the school playground. "You've been in a mood all morning

28

and you didn't even smile when Mrs Parfitt asked you to give out all the art stuff."

"I've got a headache," I reply in a flat voice. I lean against the wall and watch as Jo wipes a dribble of water from her chin.

"A headache?" Never before has someone looked so happy that their friend has a headache as Jo does at this moment. "That's great news," she says. Her hands spring forward and she clasps my shoulders as she insists she can sort it out. "I've got this bit of fabric that touched the head of a person who touched the head of a person who touched the head of—"

"Yeah, get on with it."

"Saint Teresa of Avila knew all about headaches. If I touch your head with it your headache will disappear," says Jo. "And if your headache has given you sore eyes, I've got a bit of fabric that touched the grave of a person who touched the grave of a person who touched the grave of Saint Augustine of Hippo, patron saint of sore eyes. Then again, Saint Augustine was also the patron saint of brewers so I'm not sure how useful he'll be. Anyway, come over to mine after school for a healing session."

There is no headache other than the headache Jo is beginning to give me. And I'm pretty sure that a piece of fabric that's touched a hippo can't help me with what's really wrong, which is my lack of contact from Dad. "Yes, okay, if I must," I say slowly. "But I'm only coming if you don't put holy water in my orange squash."

"I haven't got any. Dad blocked the toilet yesterday and he grabbed the bottle of holy water and used it as a container for the soggy toilet roll taken from the bowl. I wasn't very happy."

"I bet you weren't." I lift my body off the wall.

"It wasn't so much about losing the holy water, as the fact that he didn't ask me first. If he had, I would have directed him to pray to Saint Jude Thaddaeus. Because once Dad has blocked the toilet, he needs help from the patron saint of desperate cases."

Mum texts me back to say she doesn't mind me going to Jo's, which is just as well because we're already in Jo's bedroom and Jo is pressing a plastic card with a scrap of fabric inside onto my forehead. It feels cool against my skin but other than that I can't say it has made me feel any better. To make Jo happy, I stare at her wall poster of Saint Aloysius Gonzaga with his eyes raised to heaven. Then I roll my eyeballs back before snapping them forward again as if I'm healed. My acting skills aren't all that, because Jo isn't convinced.

"I don't think this is about a headache at all," says Jo, setting the card on her bedside table. "There is something else you're not telling me. By the way, friends don't keep secrets from one another."

"Which saint told you that?"

"My mother, but she's not exactly a saint." Jo folds her arms and blocks my view of Saint Aloysius Gonzaga. "You should tell me your problems."

I open my school bag and make this huge deal of pulling out a book and then pretending to read it. "I don't have any problems." I don't look at Jo because I'm so busy reading this absolutely fascinating textbook about the life cycle of a maggot.

"Your book is upside down," replies Jo, placing her hands on her hips. By the time I've righted it, she's reached into her bedside table drawer and is holding her hand aloft in a fist. "This is for you. Borrow it for a while. Give it back to me when you've got all the answers and you're healed. And you can't refuse. It's rude to say no to a present." Jo thrusts her hand open and holds it below my nostrils. There, in the centre of her palm, is a silver medal about the size of a ten-pence piece – that's if you squashed it with a steamroller and made it oblong and therefore nothing like a ten-pence piece at all. On one side, I can see an engraving of a saint who I don't recognize. Although to be honest, I don't recognize any of them.

Cross-eyed, I stare at it. "How many times do I have to tell you my head is fine?"

"Yes, and I heard you. This isn't for your head," Jo admits. "Let me introduce you to Saint Gabriel of Our Lady of Sorrows. This medal is how I got interested in relics in the first place. It was given to me by the grandma I lost playing bingo. Just after she heard the words 'Lucky seven, God's in heaven' she shouted 'House!' and keeled over. They tucked her bingo card in her coffin and Dad said she went to heaven smiling. Dad was smiling too because he inherited her winnings."

I only manage to squeak that if it isn't a medal for illness then what is it for?

"It's for someone who needs healing. It's for someone who is carrying a secret sorrow and they need a dream to come true. It's for someone like you."

CHAPTER 3

Jo told me to write a list of ten things I'd like to happen and treasure it along with the medal of Saint Gabriel of Our Lady of Sorrows. I said I couldn't write a list because it would be silly, but she said if I wrote a list Saint Gabriel would read it and heal me by making one of my dream s come true.

"Do not make the list completely ridiculous," she warned.

"Why?" I asked. "Is it because saints can't work miracles?"

"Oh, Dan." Jo shook her head with the look of a weary mastermind on all matters religious. "You know nothing of their mystical ways. You cannot pick them up, ask them for things and then put them down again. Again, I repeat, do not ask for the Crown Jewels because Saint Gabriel will not get them for you. Pick ten things he can do and he'll choose one from the list of ten and make it happen. It will be the most important one."

"How will he know which one is most important?"

Jo listened carefully then punched at her heart. "He knows because he can see inside you."

I figure out that if he can see inside me then there's no point in writing a list, but I don't tell Jo.

1. Money
2. A new sister who doesn't say horrible things
3. A dog with a strong stomach
4. An email
5. A new bike
6. A swimming pool full of chocolate cereal
7. To go to a school for wizards instead of Our Lady of the Portal
8. To live at 221b Baker Street
9. My own rocket called Hope 1
10. A dad

I fold the list around Saint Gabriel, then place him under my bed in a treasure chest on my toy pirate island. I say, "I'm not doing this because I believe you can heal me or anything. I don't. And if I'm a teeny bit sad it's because I've got a lot of homework to do and nothing else. Anyway, I'm doing this so Jo will shut up about me needing help." I pause. "But if you could...nah..." Then I spill out, "If you could see your way to making Dad send me an email, then that would be okay."

I rush over and fire up the computer.

No email.

Thin splinters of anger drive into my heart as I click on the mouse at least ten times. I even double-check that I used the right email address. Of course I did. I look in the spam folder – Dad's not there either. It is now a fact that my cunning plan to make contact with Dad has failed and he's ignoring me. So is Saint Gabriel by the looks of things.

The second email I send isn't quite as chatty as the first. I tell Dad I've been getting loads of gold stars at school and if he'd like to know more he has to email me back. Yes, I realize he is a celebrity and therefore a busy man but I hope he has time to contact his only son. With a finger like a speeding bullet, I hit send and go downstairs for those potato alphabet letters that Mum's always getting with her staff discount from Aladdin's Supermarket.

Big Dave is sitting at the table with a potato ⊗ clenched between his teeth. "Sit beside me," he says, swallowing it and pulling out a chair. Today is Tuesday and for the last three months Big Dave has been eating with us on a Tuesday. I don't mind because Mum always makes sure we have a good pudding when he's here. On the days he's not here we get limp tubes of yogurt, but on Tuesdays we get puddings straight from the big freezers at Aladdin's. To be honest, it's not only about my stomach. I like Big Dave because he makes Mum happy. For a long time after Dad left we were all sad. Then I got a dog but Mum got nothing. When Big Dave turned up he was as good as a puppy for her because she started laughing again. That's when I got my old mum back.

"Want some more alphabet shapes?" says Mum, offering round the bowl.

Big Dave manages to spell ℕ⓪ with the alphabet shapes left on his plate and shows this to Mum.

I almost fall off my chair laughing but then have to stop abruptly when Ninja Grace starts sighing and letting her eyeballs do a three-sixty. When she's like this it means she's about to go off on one. Ten seconds later, I can report, she does.

"The recession hasn't hit you," says Grace,

putting a ⓠ in her mouth and letting it squelch through her teeth.

Big Dave scratches at the tattoo on his left arm, leaving tiny traces of grease on the big inked heart. Then he shrugs, flexes his arm and goes back to mopping up his leftover brown sauce with some garlic bread. The tattooed heart pumps and, underneath, the thin scroll saying *Caroline 1973* wobbles.

"What I'm trying to say is that you're so busy you've only got one or two evenings free per week. So the recession has passed you by." Satisfied, Grace picks up an ⓞ and puts it between her lips before sucking it in. "You must have a lot of commitments that stop you seeing Mum."

This conversation is going in a direction I don't like, and it doesn't help when Grace's foot connects with my shinbone. I disguise the agony by pretending I'm choking on a ⓑ. Grace didn't have to break my tibia for me to realize what she's getting at. A few days ago, Nina Biddolpho the newsagent told me Big Dave was married and had a little boy. "Heard it through the grapevine, innit," said Nina. "Don't know much about the kid. But that's what the grapevine told me." As I'd pondered how big this grapevine must be, she told me the name of Big Dave's wife.

"Caz, innit," she said.

I didn't have to be Sherlock Holmes to work out that Caz was short for Caroline and *Caroline 1973* were the words lovingly inked on Big Dave's bulging bicep. All the pieces of the jigsaw started to fit. Big Dave couldn't be with Mum every night of the week because he was still with his wife, Caroline. I'd told Grace. We'd jumped to conclusions. Well, she did really. She was on a super-sized trampoline with springs on her feet, she was jumping so high. Grace said she knew it all along. Big Dave, it seems, was too good to be true.

From this point on, Ninja Grace was out to get Big Dave. Apparently, he was Mr Wrong and not Mr Right. I wanted to give him a chance but Grace said no, men wanted to have their cake and eat it. To be honest, I thought that sounded okay but Grace said it wasn't.

"Big Dave," Grace continues, sticking her fingernail in between her teeth. "The heart of a cheater is like one of those hollow chocolate Easter eggs." Grace makes one long hairy slug with her eyebrows. "It's empty. Mum doesn't like that. She's had it happen before and expects more. Frankly, she deserves better."

A light bulb flashes above Big Dave's head as he realizes what she's talking about. He touches his nose knowingly as I crunch down in my chair. "Don't you worry, pet, I'll make sure I don't buy your mother a hollow egg."

Grace starts and her bottom lip quivers. "I wasn't talking about eggs," she says. "What I actually meant…"

To stop Grace going any further I jump into the conversation and begin talking about all the different types of chocolates you can get in Easter eggs. Praline. Fudge. Caramel swirls. Orange creams. By the time I get to sticky toffee, Grace's eyes have turned into razors and her heel connects with my other shinbone. I let out this *"Yeeouch"*, which Mum takes to mean *yuk* and that I don't like sticky toffee much. I do, but at this moment I'm more worried that Grace has put an end to my premiership football career.

To save my shins from further injury I announce I've got to take Charles Scallybones for a walk. Mum thinks about protesting but Scallybones comes to the rescue. He starts stretching his mouth and yawning. This is usually a signal that the sick express is fast approaching. Mum says she'll save me a piece of sticky toffee pudding for when I get back. I'm about to say I'd like that very much when she says actually she won't bother, because she's just remembered I'm not a fan of sticky toffee.

To be honest, I'm still thinking about how I can get Ninja Grace back when Charles Scallybones stops and pees up the side of the Paradise scout hut. Usually this isn't a problem as it's one of his ten nightly pee stops, but tonight there's someone in a white dressing gown resting by the open door. Tonight of all nights, Charles Scallybones's bladder is holding a yellow swimming pool and when I try to drag him away he resists and pees some more. Dressing Gown Man says when my dog is quite finished using the hut as a toilet, maybe I'd like to watch what's going on inside. Maybe even join in.

Watch what? Join in where? Nothing good can come of watching people in dressing gowns. I hear a grunt from inside the hut and consider running away – right up to the point where Charles Scallybones pees on Dressing Gown Man's feet. After that I feel sort of obliged to do what he tells me.

When I get inside I see the small wooden hut is full of more Dressing Gown People, all different shapes and sizes, and all kneeling on the floor. At first I think they're praying, but then they all jump up and start punching the living daylights out of the air. Mind you, I reckon I could punch air, if I had to.

Startled by what's happening, Charles Scallybones stops chewing the black belt he found discarded on the floor. He stares up at me, eyes like wet buttons, and whimpers. Hugging the edges of the hall, I try to drag him back towards the exit. That's when I hear someone hissing my name, but trying to disguise it as a grunt. I look around, ping-pong-ball eyed. Another hissy grunt follows. Turns out it's coming from my mate Christopher. He gives me a little wave as a woman instructor shouts at him to concentrate on the five tenets of tae kwon do.

"Yes, we have a visitor, but that doesn't mean you can forget courtesy, integrity, perseverance, self-control and indomitable spirit," she shouts. I consider sticking my hand up and asking if they drink indomitable spirits down the precinct on a Friday night, but think better of it when she screams that it means never giving up. Trust me, I think the men at the precinct never give up their spirits either.

After watching for ten minutes I accept that Christopher is a master at this air-fighting. What's more, there's this sheen of sweat on his forehead, so it's not as easy as I first thought. He catches my eye a few times before doing these kicky-flicky foot snaps. I imagine they're actually called something more impressive, but I can't understand a word the instructor is saying. Anyway, I don't have time to try and figure it out, because Charles Scallybones appears to be having a fight of his own with the discarded black belt. And now it has a wound the size of the Eurotunnel. (By the way, it's not really the size of a tunnel. That is me exaggerating for dramatic effect. According to Mrs Parfitt, this is an example of *hyperbole*.)

Realizing we might have to pay for the destroyed belt, Charles Scallybones and I run away at the speed of light. (Or maybe it's greased lightning. I can't decide which. Anyway, both are hyperbole.)

When I get home, things go from bad to worse. For a start, Charles brings up some black threads. And, instead of lovely sticky toffee pudding, Mum has left me a tube of yogurt on a plate in the kitchen. Then Grace grabs me and pins me against the wall in the bathroom. She waves her toothbrush in my face. "Why did you let him off the hook?" Minty foam spills from her mouth as if she's a rabid dog. "We could have told Mum the truth earlier. Big Dave is just like Dad. Do you want to end up sitting on the stairs while they're in the kitchen with Mum screaming about *Caroline 1973*?" Grace stalks up and down the bathroom, which takes about 0.001 seconds. Every so often she blows out clouds of peppermint.

"Big Dave seems alright," I mutter. "He got me that planet mobile."

"You're easily bought." Grace snaps a strand of dental floss from the container. "You need to get your priorities right. Big Dave is not going to be a good substitute father because he's just like our own father and our own father is as much use as a waterproof teabag." Grace slides the floss through the gaps in her teeth.

"Indomitable spirit," I mutter, folding my arms.

"You what?" asks Grace, a jungle vine of floss dangling from her mouth.

I tell Grace it's nothing, but its meaning sticks in my head: never giving up. And I'm never giving up on Dad. Yes, he might have run off with Busty Babs, but there has to be more to it. Mum always says there are two sides to every story. And a part of me is clinging to the idea that Dad didn't abandon us and I'm going to send him email number three and then he'll prove it. When Dad replies I'm going to make Grace Hope eat her words, and this time they won't be alphabet shapes from Aladdin's.

My third email is unlike the other two. For a start, I don't bother telling Dad all the things going on at school. No more *I've got a gold star and I'm really clever* stuff. Instead, I write the whole email in caps and ask him why he left us and didn't send birthday cards. The birthday cards thing is important.

When I was eight, I wanted a card from Dad that said **It's great when you're eight**. I hoped it would have a red rocket with *Hope 1* on it. There would have been an astronaut wearing a bubble helmet looking out of the little round rocket window, and inside Dad would have written a message saying he was sorry he couldn't be with me. He'd say it was because he was a journalist on a secret mission to the Back of Beyond and he hoped I understood.

No birthday card ever turned up.

On my ninth birthday, I hoped for a card from Dad that said It's fine to be nine. It would have had a shiny bike on it, the colour of a red admiral's wings, and a boy freewheeling down a hill with sparks coming from his tyres because he's zooming so fast.

Again there was no card.

The following year there was still no card from Dad, and on my last birthday, when I wanted a card that said IT'S HEAVEN TO BE ELEVEN, I got nothing more than a flyer telling me to get down to Jason's Donervan and try out their new royally delicious feast, The King Kebab.

I finish my email by telling Dad I want him to respond within twenty-four hours, or else. I hit send.

Within ten seconds, an email from the TV station pops into my inbox.

There is nothing between Dad and our future together except the click of a mouse. My stomach twists and knots as if a magician is making a balloon giraffe out of it. For ages I stare at the screen, before screwing up my courage. This is it, I tell myself. This is the beginning of our new lives together. I open the email and inhale. Two seconds later I feel water leak down my cheek and splatter onto my lap. When I look down, I notice my tears have left a stain in the shape of a broken heart.

CHAPTER 4

Dad didn't reply to my email after all. Instead, my unanswered email was bounced back. I don't mind admitting that I'm confused and no longer feel quite as confident as I did before. At this point I bring out the pirate island and retrieve Saint Gabriel and my list and I tell him he's failed on getting me an email.

"Strike one," I scold, flicking the medal with my fingers. "But I'll let you off if you can get me into a school for wizards." I get a pencil and draw a line through number four on my list and put everything back inside the treasure chest and then I take the plastic skull-and-crossbones flag and stick it on top to show my anger.

Dad, it seems, has poured poison on the little tree I was growing inside my soul. Slowly the leaves begin to wilt. Without hesitation I send him another email. Who knows, maybe I'm having an out-of-body experience. Mum once said a character in an old TV soap called *Dallas* died and then turned up in the shower and everything that had happened before was just a dream. So I run into the bathroom, climb into the shower, count to ten, jump back out and sit down at the computer again. Nope. Not a dream. Because the email I just sent to Dad has pinged back at me, unanswered.

That night I don't sleep too well. I have a strange dream that I'm in Paradise. Only it's not Paradise estate as I know it. Instead, I'm under a tree and leaves are falling on me like emeralds and Saint Gabriel's medal is the sun. At first it feels amazing and I hold my outstretched hands to the sky, catching the gem leaves as they fall. Some spill through my fingers but others are brittle. A cloud passes over Saint Gabriel and it grows dark as more emeralds shower me and I want to call for help, only I have no voice. That's when someone reaches out and, although I can't see the person's face, I feel the grasp of their fingers on mine. For a second I'm confused and want to pull away. But their grip is firm and somewhere deep inside I know I have to trust them. When I wake up, I swear I can still feel the warmth of their hand in mine.

Walking to school the next morning is horrible. In the ten minutes it takes me to reach the gates I've decided I might as well score number seven off the list. Our Lady of the Portal isn't rising from mists of magic like a school for wizards – instead it's sitting like a huge grey prison dumped in a gravel pit of utter misery. To make matters worse, one of the prisoners is acting weird. Christopher wants to know why I didn't stay longer and watch him do tae kwon do. But just as I'm about to open my mouth, Jo says that she needs a chat, just the two of us. Unfortunately, this private chat doesn't amount to more than a discussion on how Saint Gabriel died of tuberculosis, aged twenty-four. From the corner of my eye I notice Christopher get up and sit beside Kevin Cummings. He says very loudly that it's not nice to be left out by people he thought were his friends.

After lunch Christopher is still in a mood. He doesn't even crack a smile when Mrs Parfitt asks us to sit down because she has exciting news. "I have a new project for you to work on," says Mrs Parfitt, looking around at twenty-eight not-so-eager faces. "We're going to start Project Eco Everywhere."

Kevin Cummings pipes up that that's PEE for short and Mrs Parfitt tells him that if she wants an opinion she'll give it to him. "Yes, Miss," he says, slumping back in his chair.

Apparently, Project Eco Everywhere is going to be our opportunity to highlight how much we throw away and how we can actually create something really special. Mrs Parfitt calls it zero to hero, which means we're taking items no one wants and using them to create an outfit immortalizing someone important in our lives. When we're finished, not only are we going to model these outfits on a Project Eco Everywhere catwalk, but at a later stage we're going to raffle them off to make money to donate to local projects that help educate people about litter.

"You can bring in old egg cartons, cereal packets, clothing, empty pie cases and wrapping foil or whatever else you find. Show me you can turn rubbish into something good. I want to see your hero emerge."

"From the dump," whispers Kevin Cummings.

"When I say hero, I think it would be nice if you look close to home. Do you have a parent or a sibling who could be your hero? I don't want obvious superheroes from the movies. I want real heroes, if at all possible," say Mrs Parfitt. "If you can't think of a family member, pick someone else you look up to. And remember you'll be wearing this on a catwalk, so big and bold is the way to go."

"A catwalk?" yelps Jo. "I'm going to be a supermodel—"

"Wearing an old steak and kidney pie tin," shouts Kevin. As Mrs Parfitt approaches him he slumps back in his chair again and pretends to zip his lips.

Mrs Parfitt stops, looks around and says, "The Project Eco Everywhere show is going to take place at the Amandine Hotel instead of at school. This is because they've offered the ballroom for free if we advertise them in our brochure. Isn't it exciting? And..." The words hang tantalizingly in the air. "There might be a big surprise. I can't tell you what it is yet because it isn't fully organized. But let's just say that you will want to do well on this project."

I make a mental list of family members I could turn into heroes for PEE. It doesn't take long. There is Mum or Ninja Grace... I think for a millisecond before deciding I'm going to do Dad instead. All right, so he's not exactly top of my hero list at the moment, but this could be my new bright idea to bring him back into my life. I don't know precisely how this bright idea will make that happen, but I'm working on it.

Christopher suddenly mutters that he's going to do his dad too. For some reason I'm surprised. It's not that I didn't think he had a family – it's just that he's never mentioned them before. When I try to make conversation by asking him what his dad is like, he says that he's like everyone else's dad. It's on the tip of my tongue to say that I doubt it.

"You're doing what?" snorts Ninja Grace when I tell her about PEE. She's waiting, arm-in-arm with Stan, at the school gates. "Did I hear you right? You're making a hero outfit from rubbish and then modelling it on a catwalk. Sounds like a freak show to me."

I shove my hands in my pockets and start walking. "Yeah, it's all about showing how much we chuck away and how we can make something special from it."

"You can have a pair of my laddered tights for ninety-nine pence. Cheaper than what they charged me at the pound shop," quips Grace.

Stan laughs at Grace's joke, strokes the face fungus growing on his upper lip and watches as at least one whole digestive in crumb-form drops out.

"I'm making Dad my hero," I say.

There's this dramatic silence. Actually, I think the birds stop tweeting. The world stops turning and all the rivers subside, leaving fish flapping on dry riverbeds. The sun disappears and I'm left standing in a vortex.

"You are *not* making Dad your hero," squeals Grace.

Word ninja aims her samurai at my heart!

Stan looks awkward, which to be fair isn't too far removed from how he usually looks, and his tongue pokes about for another 'tache digestive. After that he makes some excuse about getting home to watch his favourite quiz show. When Stan turns left at the fork in the road, Grace blurts out that she thinks I'm delusional.

"I don't think so," I say, scuffing my toes along the pavement.

"You see. You're deluding yourself about deluding yourself." Grace stomps alongside me. "Just because you've seen Dad on telly doesn't mean he's a hero."

"Yeah, but..." I say.

Grace stops and looks at me. "No buts, unless you're a goat."

"But I'm allowed to have a dad," I reply.

"Sure you are. Don't t.   though. Don't expect him .   word ninja storms off towa.   shouting, "You're a mentalist!"

I trail after her, muttering how
know one.

As soon as I turn my key in the lock an.   .le
hallway, Grace calls me upstairs. But she's n. .n her
bedroom, she's in mine. When I tell her she's in
the wrong room, a villainous smile plays on her lips
and she lifts up a small slip of paper and dangles it
in front of me, then swings it like the pendulum of
a clock.

"I knew you were up to no good, and this proves
it." The paper wafts in front of me and my eyes
follow it.

Trying to grab it, I shout, "I'm telling Mum you
were snooping in my bedroom."

"Oh no you're not. For your information, I had to
come in here to check on that mutt of yours because
he was barfing up that toy pirate you left on the
carpet. Did you want me to leave him with a plastic
cutlass jammed between his canines?"

"No," I reply. "But you were still being nosy and
going through my stuff. Mum won't be happy with
you."

"Get over yourself. You wouldn't dare tell Mum

want to know what it was about and
be my duty to tell her you've been emailing
Dad." In this battle of threats, Grace is the winner
and she knows it.

"I thought about emailing Dad," I say, "but I
changed my mind. I'm not going to bother."

Grace rips the paper into tiny bits. "Correct
answer! And if I were you I wouldn't leave Dad's
email address taped to the front of your computer
again. It's rather obvious. You're definitely not
going to email him, are you?"

"I promise I will not email Dad," I return.
Satisfied, Grace asks me to hold out my hand, which
I do. She sets the foamy, sick-covered pirate in my
palm. Then she opens her other hand and lets Dad's
email address flutter down like confetti.

"Look," Grace says, triumphant. "Your pirate is
on the island of broken dreams and hey, it's
snowing."

Despite being stuck with the worst sister in the
world, I'm not going to break my promise to her.

So I won't be emailing Dad again.

Next time, I'm going to see him face-to-face.

I'm going to be like Sherlock Holmes tracking Moriarty. This is going to take meticulous planning – even more than when I recreated the town hall from lollipop sticks. I take a piece of paper from my desk and write:

DANIEL GEORGE HOPE

AGE 11

OPERATION BASKERVILLE

(You have to use names like Baskerville because that way no one really knows what you're up to. If I wrote Operation Meeting Dad then Ninja Grace would be onto me like a bloodhound.)

The very first job of Operation Baskerville is to find Dad's address.

Thirty minutes and one very messy hallway later and I've found this ancient book that appears to have all the addresses of local people inside it. Yes, the actual addresses *plus* phone numbers. The thing weighs as much as a brick and when Mum asks me why I'm carrying the telephone directory up to my bedroom I tell her I'm going to stand on it so I can reach something at the back of my cupboard.

"Really?" Mum arches her eyebrow. "I'm surprised you can open your cupboard without an avalanche falling on your head. Well, when you've finished whatever mischief you're up to, I have an idea. Look up cleaners in the directory. I need someone to tidy this hallway. I think you'll find the person under H for Hope. First name: Daniel."

There are three people in the directory with the same name as Dad: Malcolm John Maynard. Dad doesn't have the same surname as us because Mum made sure we took her name, which I guess is kind of lucky now. Pulling out my mobile, I ring Malcolm J. Maynard number one. He says, "Wrong number, mate," and then hangs up. The second one sounds faintly Scottish and calls me "bairn", even though I tell him three times that my name is Dan. The third tells me he's always getting phone calls for that new TV presenter and everyone is really getting on his goat. His goat must be the size of the biggest Billy Goat Gruff if *everyone* is getting on it. In the end I hang up, because I have no leads *and* I have to tidy the hallway.

The whole of Operation Baskerville is in jeopardy until Big Dave makes me think otherwise. He appears on the dot of six and says he could eat a scabby dog. Mum tells him it would be wrong to eat Charles Scallybones the First so perhaps we should have a takeaway instead. Now, this is hardly riveting and has nothing whatsoever to do with Operation Baskerville, but what Big Dave says next does. Chippy chips are what Big Dave wants, from The Frying Squad to be precise. Mum says she's not eating from a place where girls wear the scent of cheap malt vinegar.

"Wok This Way it is then," says Big Dave. "The man behind the counter can lure me with a number twenty-five and the scent of sweet 'n' sour chicken balls instead."

And, thanks to Big Dave's chicken balls, I know exactly where to find Dad's address.

"So...how's it going with the medal?" whispers Jo, looking down at her list of fractions. "Do you still feel sad?"

"I never told you I felt sad in the first place," I whisper. "What's the answer to 1/7 x 1/8?"

"You didn't need to tell me, it was written all over your face."

"What, in invisible ink?" I mutter. "Is it 1/56?"

"Yes. That medal will change your life," replies Jo. "Saint Gabriel always gets results. That's what my grandma said."

"Before she died, yes," I hiss. "What's the answer to 41/3 + 41/3?"

"Grandma might have died but that wasn't the end of it. She sent me a feather, you know." Jo looks at me. "A message from her was on my list of ten things and it arrived after her funeral. Feathers are angels' calling cards. It means the dead person is up there and looking after you and they're sending you a white feather to let you know that everything will be okay."

"Jo, I hate to break this to you, but feathers come from birds' bums."

"The answer is 82/3." Jo scribbles on her test sheet and turns away from me.

"Class," says Mrs Parfitt, "I'd like to add an extra

verbal question to your test. Answer this: a group of Year Six students were working on their maths test. Their teacher noted that 3/7 were writing down the answers like good children, 2/7 were trying to figure out the answers but this involved them staring out the window, and 1/7 were looking at the clock and wishing it was over. And one person was chattering away in the middle of a test and distracting everyone else. What was the name of that one person?" Mrs Parfitt's hand bangs on my desk. I've never seen her hands close up before. Her knuckles resemble an elephant's knees.

A few people start scribbling down my name and laughing.

"Daniel Hope," she says, pointing to my test paper. "If you don't stop these cosy chats with Jo and work out the answers yourself, what score do you think you'll be getting on this paper?"

"Zero," I reply.

"Correct," Mrs Parfitt replies.

The whole matter would have been closed with Mrs Parfitt's telling-off, only I look over at Christopher and he glances up at me and then Jo. For a split second he seems embarrassed, but that's not all. Christopher also looks a bit smug, as if I deserved a telling-off for talking to Jo. But that doesn't even make sense.

At morning break I'm standing by the toilet block when Christopher walks past and throws a tennis ball against the wall. When it bounces I snap it up and hand it over to him, saying, "You were good at tae kwon do. Sorry I couldn't hang around and watch for longer but I had my dog with me."

Christopher nods but doesn't answer.

"Have I done something else to annoy you?"

"No," he replies.

"Is this about Jo? You looked sort of happy that I got into trouble because we were talking. But it's not my fault that Jo keeps jabbering on about religious relics and feathers that come from angels' bums."

Christopher bounces the tennis ball up and down, then stops and looks across at Jo.

She's slouched on a bench, with long copper waves of hair falling down past her shoulder. One sock is up and the other down and she's playing with a badge on her blazer lapel. When she senses Christopher and me looking at her, she waves. Christopher smiles back and does this ridiculous little micro finger-wave that makes him look about two.

"Hey," shouts Christopher, "come and talk to me."

Jo pulls up her sock, wanders towards us and then asks me if I want to come round to her house after school.

I shake my head. "I'm busy with Baskerville."

Jo's eyes widen. "What's that?"

I shrug and say I could tell her but then I'd have to kill her. Jo laughs and informs me that I'm missing out. She has a new plastic statue of the Virgin Mary that I've really got to see. When you switch the lights off her heart glows in the dark and if you wind up her halo she plays "Ave Maria".

"I'd like to see it," says Christopher.

And that's when I know for certain what Christopher's problem is.

CHAPTER 6

The Frying Squad sits beside the alleyway between the Paradise and Ireland estates. It is a small shop with a black and white chessboard floor and a neon-pink flying fish flashing in the window. For the past four years I haven't been allowed to go inside. Mum wouldn't even mention the name in our presence. Grace said we would catch carbohydrate scurvy if we couldn't eat chips from the chip shop but Mum didn't care and said we'd have to fur up our arteries another way. Grace told me this whole mess was thanks to Dad coming home stinking of battered sausages.

I don't remember that. The bit about battered sausages, I mean. When I think of Dad I imagine spiced apples. And I'd almost forgotten that whenever I thought there were burglars in my wardrobe, Dad would whip my plastic sword from the toy box, fling open the door and whack the inside of the wardrobe until no thief could survive. And when I thought a monster might have hidden under my bed, Dad sneaked under there to check. I don't believe in monsters any more, but then again, I'm not sure I can believe in Dad either.

Charles Scallybones scuffs my leg with his claws and then puts his nose to the chessboard, searching for food.

Charles Scallybones moves piece of fish to b1		Chip end at f2
	Slice of sausage at g7	Mushy pea at c8

"Your dog is vacuuming my floor," says the man behind the counter.

"All part of the service," I say, resting my elbows beside this huge glass jar full of prehistoric eggs. "He'll eat anything." I pause and take a deep breath. "I wondered if I could get…"

"Pollock?" he asks, scratching his chin.

"No," I reply.

"Pea fritter?" His greasy quiff wobbles.

"No."

"Cod?"

"An address for Babs," I say. I don't mention the busty bit, just in case.

"Do you want chips with that?"

Seems I'm being blackmailed. All I've got in my pocket is a button the dog ate from my blazer and then threw up in Grace's beanie, a half-eaten chewy sweet and a fifty-pence coin. (Saint Gabriel didn't help with number one on my list. I've already scored it off because I'm still broke.) Fifty pence is not enough for chips, but it is enough for a prehistoric egg from the jar saying

CHEAP AS CHIPS*
(*it's your lucky day — they're cheaper than chips).

"Pickled egg, please." I slide my coin across the counter. As he reaches for it, I pull it back and say, "Plus Babs's address. She used to work with you, I believe." (Saying "I believe" makes you sound grown up.)

Charles Scallybones has moved on to eating a corner of paper napkin on c7.

The man puts the egg specimen into a paper bag. "You'll need to eat this fast or the bottom will fall out of the bag."

"And the address?" I let him take the coin.

"It was years ago now but I think it was the end house on Swallow Street. It's near that big hill where all the children go. That's all I know and it's worth more than fifty pence."

I push the button across the counter with my index finger. "Don't spend it all at once," I say. I think about winking, only I change my mind halfway through and end up walking away with a drooping eyelid.

"Your pickled egg, I believe," the man shouts after me. "You've forgotten it." I have to turn back and pick it up from the counter.

Outside, I offer the egg to Charles Scallybones, who sniffs it and jumps away as if it's alive. A few seconds later he returns and wags his tail. Another whiff and he thinks it might just be edible. The pickled egg is swallowed whole. A moment later, the pickled egg comes back scrambled.

The hill, I tell myself as I walk back home, is not more than twenty minutes from our house. I've skateboarded down it many times. Is that where Dad has lived since he walked out? But it's so close that we could have easily bumped into each other. And if it's so close, why didn't he come and visit? I go through a whole list of possible reasons why not, but none of them amount to much. The fact remains that Dad didn't come. But it doesn't stop me going to him.

Part two of Operation Baskerville involves the *searchyourstreets* website. With Dad's address in my mind, I switch on the computer and check out Swallow Street. (A good detective does stuff like this. You don't think Sherlock Holmes would storm straight in, do you? Instead, he would prepare, plan it out and make deductions before visiting the scene.) I find the end house.

For a start, this is no Buckingham Palace x 1, let alone x 3. No fancy walls and curling iron gates. As for a flag fluttering in the wind, forget it. What this turns out to be is a normal-looking house with a neat hedge and wooden fence. To the side there's a long alleyway littered with bins. I zoom into Dad's back garden, where there are rose bushes, trees, a pathway that looks like large pebbles dotted on the lawn, a bird fountain and a wooden shed. All very ordinary for a celebrity, that's for sure.

To the right of the house, further down the road, there is a wooded area and to its side drops Skateboarding Hill, which leads down to Paradise estate. I've been in that wood a few times. Once I built a den out of cardboard in there, only it rained and I ended up walking home looking like a papier-mâché monster.

The first thing I think, as I jam my skateboard under my arm and make my way to the summit of Skateboarding Hill, is how much I want this. I didn't think it was possible to need my dad as much as I do now. Down below in the valley, November has just tipped into December and frost is spreading like a glittery disease through the streets. In the distance I can see the fairy lights around Aladdin's Supermarket, where Mum is at this very moment probably ding-dinging frozen Brussels sprouts through her scanner. Far beyond Aladdin's, just on the edge of the Paradise estate, the dark frosted fields roll away into eternity. You can't see what is beyond and although I know it's just the next town, I imagine it to be the end of the world.

Above me the inky sky has been flicked with a white paintbrush. There are zillions of tiny snow-white dots, some big, some small, some splattered.

And the crescent moon is like the tip of Ninja Grace's manicured nail. I breathe in and out. Plumes rise into the chilled air. I'm going to do this. I'm going to do it right now.

I hide my skateboard in the wood, thinking I'll pick it up on the way back home. No point in carrying it over to Dad's house. At this stage I haven't planned what I'm going to do when I get there. But that's okay. I'm going to take everything as it comes. If I decide to ring the doorbell and wait for Dad I will. If I want to ring the doorbell and hide then I can do that too. In fact, I can do anything I want, because I'm the master of Operation Baskerville.

I am invincible.

I am a genius.

I am unstoppable.

I am scared.

Dad's house sits on the junction between one row of houses and the beginning of another. Just a glance at it and my stomach lurches. At first I walk past, whistling. Whistling is never suspicious, oh no. Next door, the neighbour's curtains move and I've been spotted, so I run into the alleyway at the side of Dad's house. As I rest my head against the cool shadows I hear a cat meow and footsteps coming towards me. A bin bag rustles. I haven't got time to wonder what Sherlock Holmes would do. Instead, this is what Dan Hope does: I climb up onto a bin and throw myself over the nearest fence and into a garden. Behind me I hear a bin lid lift and the thump of rubbish. The footsteps dissolve.

There is good news and bad news. The good news: I have avoided being discovered lurking in the alleyway outside Dad's house. The bad news: I am now lurking in Dad's garden. Eventually I sneak down the garden path. And here's the odd thing: when I was on *searchyourstreets* I didn't see the trampoline by the fence. Nor did I spot the small football net or the discarded plastic water pistol. They look out of place in the garden, as if they don't belong.

At the point where I reach the trampoline, the kitchen light goes on and I can hear a key rattling in the back door lock.

"Hello?" A voice cuts through the darkness.

Sweat spouts from my scalp and a small river snakes through my hair as I run down the garden and throw my body against the shadowy side of the shed.

"If someone is hiding in the garden I'll ring the police. I've got speed dial on my mobile."

I hug the dark, trying not to breathe.

It's hard not to breathe. Breathing's sort of important.

I know I can't hide here for ever and I pray for the person to go back into the house. And I think they might have done if I hadn't just then seen a huge hairy monster rise from the depths of the garden path and throw itself against my leg. I kick out and my trainer connects with a furball. It lets out an almighty hiss that breaks the silence. To tell you the truth, that's the moment when it all goes wrong and I forget I'm supposed to be breathing like a sleeping baby and start chuffing like an old steam train climbing Mount Everest.

The cat, because that's all it is, patters away from me as the dark figure runs towards me, screaming and hollering how they knew there was an intruder in the garden. "If you're paparazzi there's going to be trouble. There are laws against this sort of stuff. You can't spy on a minor just because my dad is famous."

My dad?

Your dad?

Our dad?

CHAPTER 7

There are about ten million thoughts going through my head but the main one is RUN. This boy races towards me, arms flailing like Catherine wheels. As he approaches, I realize he's about fifteen and built like a bulldog, if that bulldog was actually made of bricks.

I bomb towards him as if I'm a superhero with wings on his feet. Speed is mine and I'm going to get past Catherine Wheel Boy. My trainers are moving so fast they're a blur. I'm halfway up the pebble path when his toe connects with my ankle. He loses his balance, which is no bad thing, because suddenly there's this *ooooof* sound coming from my stomach and I'm less superhero, more the boy with broken wings sprawled on the path.

"Paparazzi paparazzi paparazzi," he shouts quickly, which is impressive since it sounds like a tongue-twister.

Swallowing back the pain, I jump up and run away from him, leap onto the trampoline and boing up and down as fast as I can. On the final bounce I'm on top of the fence, then over the other side and onto a rubbish bin. After that, I jump to the ground and half run, half hobble down the alleyway and into Swallow Street.

"Loser," screams the boy and I can hear a thud as he kicks the fence.

Reaching Skateboarding Hill is the only target in my mind. The pain is forgotten as I run through the wood, and I don't stop or look back in case Catherine Wheel Boy is behind me. I find the spot where I hid my skateboard and drag it out from under the brambles, then run through the wood with it in my clutches. When I reach the top of the hill, I risk a backward glance. The boy hasn't followed me. With a quick flick my skateboard goes down onto the pathway and I jump on and whoosh down Skateboarding Hill, grateful for those high-performance bearings. At the bottom I dive off and land face down in the long grass.

I lie there for ages asking myself the same question.

How could my dad be his dad?

Frosted blades of grass tickle my cheeks and the Paradise estate is on its side. I thought I was the only boy in the universe who could say Malcolm Maynard was my dad. But I can hear Catherine Wheel Boy's words inside my head and my eyes see dark sponge clouds gliding across the horizon. I found Dad's house. Operation Baskerville was a success. A tear eases out and runs along the side of my head and seeps into the earth. I think I'm a genius. Another tear follows. I think I am invincible. A third tear follows the path of the first two. I think I'm lonely.

An hour later I find myself under my duvet without knowing what steps I took to get there. The glow-in-the-dark stars light the ceiling; five-pointed beacons of happiness. It hurts to look at them, so I close my eyes. When Mum got home from the supermarket she shouted up that she'd brought back some slightly stale biscuits that they couldn't sell. Even then I didn't leave my bedroom to get any.

That night I dream of the Paradise estate again. It's the same dream as before: the one where I'm standing beneath the Dad tree. This time the Saint

Gabriel medal has turned into the moon and the leaves from the tree fall like rubies from heaven. At first I catch them, but they shatter and fall around me like petals falling from a blood-red rose. They blanket the ground before building up until they reach my knees and then my waist. I stumble and fall below a scarlet river, my fingers the only thing visible. The hand, when it comes, fills me with hope. From nowhere it grasps my fingers and pulls me upwards. I wake up thinking of Dad.

"The monster appears for breakfast," says Grace, shovelling toast into her mouth. "You look a right mess."

Mum looks up at me and then her eyes skip away. Her fingers wrap around a mug of steaming tea and occasionally she takes a sip. "Do you feel rough too?"

I shrug and sit down at the table.

"Something I ate hasn't agreed with me," says Mum. A volcanic burp rumbles in her ribcage and she puts a fist to her mouth before it explodes. "Sorry."

As I pour the last of the chocolate cereal into a bowl I mentally cross number six off my list. Saint

Gabriel is never going to get me a swimming pool full of these babies.

"Too many biscuits," Mum sighs. "I knew I shouldn't have eaten the entire packet myself."

Mum's face is the colour of a dolphin's flipper. If I put her in my grey school jumper you wouldn't be able to tell where Mum's skin begins and the jumper ends. Usually Mum is never ill, so it's a surprise when she says she'll have a little lie-down before her shift at Aladdin's. When I ask if I can help, she smiles and says I could look in her handbag for some indigestion tablets and bring them up to her with a glass of water.

"Ooh, Mr Suck-Up from Suck-Up Street, Suck-Up Town," says Grace as Mum disappears up the stairs. She's just jealous because I thought to ask Mum if I could help, which makes me Number One child. As I stick my tongue out, Grace screeches, "Ugh! Chocolate puke."

Mum's pink sequined bag is tucked neatly under the coats in the hallway. I unzip it and look inside. This is the same as discovering one of the mysteries of the universe. I'm like that bloke going into Tutankhamun's tomb for the first time. What am I going to discover? Will there be treasure?

At first sight, nothing exciting. No mini gyro flyer or finger skateboard, and definitely no pick 'n' mix sweets. Neatly folded up and hiding at the bottom of the bag is a booklet. I take it out and sit on the bottom stair, smoothing the paper across my lap. There is a questionnaire inside and it's from our local hospital, The Princess Rose. And I know it's wrong to read other people's stuff but there you go. There's only room for one saint in this house and that's Gabriel. So the first question is:

1. Your boobs are:
   a) Perky
   b) Lumpy
   c) Sore and prickly

Prickly makes me think of hedgehogs and I'm quite certain Mum doesn't have two of those in her bra. But she has circled b) and c). Question number two makes no sense whatsoever.

2. Is there:
   a) No blood
   b) Spotting
   c) Heavy blood

Mum has circled a) this time, which is the only answer that doesn't make me gag.

Question three has me completely stumped. In

fact, it might as well be written in French for all the sense it makes.

3. Describe your symptoms:
   a) Fit, happy and full of life
   b) Heartburn, achy, uncomfortable
   c) Moody, exhausted and always going
      to the toilet

Again, Mum has circled two: b) and c). I know she's heading towards forty in a fast car, but surely it's not time to give up on life just yet. Mrs Nunkoo from down the road is eighty-six and she's probably more a) than Mum.

The last question isn't really a question at all. It says if you circled more than two b)s or c)s then you need to ring the clinic to make an appointment. Mum has underlined the phone number, twice. In red ink, no less.

I fold the booklet up again and hide it back in her bag. Not what I was expecting to find when told to get the indigestion tablets. From upstairs I hear the drift of Mum's voice asking me to hurry up before the acid starts eating her stomach alive. "I'm coming," I call back.

At school I keep thinking about secrets. Mum's sick and keeping it secret and Dad's living with Catherine Wheel Boy and keeping it secret. Big Dave is living with *Caroline 1973* and keeping it a secret. I'm worried about everyone and keeping it a secret. And Grace is just Grace. Earlier I shoved Saint Gabriel in my blazer pocket and brought him to school with me.

"Is number nine out of the question?" I whisper into my pocket. "If I had a rocket I could fly to the moon and escape all these problems on earth. At least send me a rocket if you can't do the other things."

"Daniel Hope, can you please pay attention?" says Mrs Parfitt.

"I suppose I could settle for number eight if I can't have the rocket," I mutter under my breath. "Number eight would be mega." I idly scribble my new address on my notebook.

Daniel George Hope
22lb Baker Street
London

"Whoever is whispering, please stop." Mrs Parfitt, with her big bird beak, peers in my direction and then she puffs up her chest until the buttons on her blouse strain against the fabric. "This is more important than your inane chit-chat. This is Project Eco Everywhere news. Now, as you know, we're not doing a nativity play this year, as Project Eco Everywhere is going to take its place."

"Awww..." says Kevin Cummings. "I wanted to be Joseph."

"The donkey, more like," says Jo.

"Quiet, please," replies Mrs Parfitt. "This is going to be unique. Perhaps not quite as unique as the story of Jesus' birth, that I'll grant you, but special nonetheless. If you're missing the nativity angle, I can promise you we're going to have some stars hanging from the ceiling in the hotel."

"We'll need a few shepherds too," says Kevin.

"There will be no shepherds," Mrs Parfitt says flatly. "Unless your hero is an actual shepherd, although I find this hard to believe."

"Nah," replies Kevin. "I'm doing my dad and he's very important because he works for the Queen."

"In what capacity?" asks Mrs Parfitt. You can tell she's impressed because her eyes are twice the size they normally are.

"Dad works in Her Majesty's Revenue and Customs. In fact, I bet he collects your tax, Miss."

"Oh," says Mrs Parfitt and her eyes shrink back to little rabbit droppings. "Well, that's very interesting but I think we should move on." She claps her hands. "Okay, for today's task I want you to write a poem about your hero and this will help you visualize them and perhaps give you ideas for your costume. Yes, Kevin, what is it now?"

"What if I swapped Dad for the man who owns the pawn shop?"

"Why would you want to do that? Is he your hero?"

"Not really, Miss, but he could bring gold like one of the wise men. There's loads of it in his shop window."

"There is no nativity, Kevin. I thought I made that perfectly clear. This is about your hero. You can write an ode, a sonnet, a shape poem, a haiku or whatever else you like, but I want to be pleasantly surprised. If it will help, I looked up the definition of a hero and it's a person who is admired for their noble qualities. Now it's up to you."

"Can I do the Virgin Mary?" asks Jo. "I was going to do my mum but then I thought about how much I admire Mary and how she's the most famous mother in the world."

Mrs Parfitt sighs and replies, "If you really must. But make sure she jumps off the page at me."

"Sounds scary," whispers Jo, pulling out her notebook and drawing a halo.

It *is* scary. How the heck am I supposed to write a poem about Dad being my hero when I've just realized I don't actually know much about him? In the end, I manage to write something, but I'm not sure it says much about Dad's noble qualities.

My Dad: A poem

There once was a man called Dad
Who made me incredibly mad
I sent him some mail
It came back as fail
And now I'm really quite sad

I glance over at Christopher's work and instead of writing a poem he's drawing this picture of his dad. In it, his dad is wearing his heart on his sleeve.

"Christopher." Mrs Parfitt glides over to his desk. I knew this was coming. "All very commendable but

I didn't ask you to draw your hero. I asked you to write a poem about them. Instead of *drawing* hearts, why not write it *from the heart*?" I quickly put my arm over my work in case she sees what I've written. "If you're stuck on what to write about your father, I suggest you try writing about your mother instead."

"I don't have a mother," says Christopher, playing with his fingers.

Later, when I ask Christopher if he meant what he said in class, he pretends not to hear me. When I repeat the question he gives me a death glare and says he was only messing around so he could draw pictures instead of doing work.

I know he's lying but I don't know why.

CHAPTER 8

The zombies are taking over the world and Big Dave thinks it's hilarious. As a zombie man and his zombie dog wander down the dark alley searching for human flesh, I scoop handfuls of popcorn and shovel it into my mouth. Big Dave says he's watched this movie many times and it always cracks him up.

"Boys, zombies, dogs, popcorn – an unbeatable combination," says Big Dave, dropping the kernels down his throat.

These four things make me happy, which is a big deal since I'd been feeling properly fed up after the Dad incident two nights ago. Big Dave arrived at just the right moment with the movie and a popcorn bucket. I look over at him and he tells me to keep watching the screen because the best bit is coming up. He warns me to watch the zombie with the crazy eyes.

"That's all of them," I say and then I laugh.

I can't help but like Big Dave. Despite knowing he has a wife and child, he's fun to be around. No matter how many times I tell myself not to enjoy his company, I can't do it. While he snorts at a zombie, I wonder if he hugs his wife the way he hugs Mum: all open-armed and smiling, then deep and comforting, with his fingers knotting her hair. I wonder if *Caroline 1973* pats him on his bald head the way Mum does.

"There are more zombies now. They're behind you," shouts Big Dave. "The zombie dog wants a human bone. Look out! They're getting into your house."

"Where do you live?" I mumble through pillows of popcorn, but I keep my eyes on the TV screen.

Big Dave doesn't look at me. "Over in the Ireland estate." He laughs and points at a zombie falling through a window before rolling down a flight of stairs.

"The houses are nice there," I say.

"Yup, they are," says Big Dave, adding, "but I'm only renting at the moment."

"Have you been there long?" I ask.

"Not long. We've moved around a bit, I suppose."

We, not I. Big Dave has just slipped up. Not that he's noticed, because he's too busy shouting at the man in the movie that there are zombies behind him. Big Dave says this bit gets him every time. "It's ridiculous," he says. "How can that bloke not know there are twenty zombies shuffling along behind his back? The mumbling and grunting should give it away."

"Where's your wife?" I don't know why I suddenly blurt it out, but I do. It's as though my tongue freaked out and said the exact thing I was thinking in my head.

Big Dave chokes on a bit of popcorn and bangs his chest with a fist. "Sorry, popcorn went the wrong way. It's lethal stuff. I know of a woman who broke her back tooth because of the hard bits. Maybe I should give it up too before it gets stuck in my windpipe." Big Dave gets up from the sofa and walks ridiculously fast towards the kitchen, saying he needs a beer before he pops his clogs from popcorn.

Big Dave is funny like that. Only I'm not laughing, because the zombies have left the house and made it to the shopping mall, and my big moment has gone. Gone but not forgotten. I'm already ahead on Operation Baskerville so, in theory, I could add another mystery to my list. This is the brightest of my bright ideas. I mean, how difficult could it be to find out more about *Caroline 1973*?

Operation Reichenbach is born.

Reichenbach Falls is where Sherlock Holmes takes on his arch-enemy, Moriarty. I read it in Dad's Sherlock book and it was so exciting that a bit of chocolate wafer dropped from my mouth onto the page and now it acts as a brown bookmark. Of course, I'm not saying I'm likely to end up beside a waterfall, fighting tooth and nail. And I'm not saying Big Dave might be like Moriarty or that he's toying with Mum's affections, but if the deerstalker fits... Either way, if Caroline 1973 is out there, then I want to know all about her.

In a Sherlock mystery there are lots of clues. My first Operation Reichenbach clue is the one from Nina Biddolpho, who told me that Big Dave has a wife called Caz and a small son. Nina Biddolpho knows everything, what with her being a newsagent and gossiping to hundreds of people a day. You can hardly think you're going to sneeze in Paradise without her offering to sell you a box of tissues.

I know Nina was absolutely certain about Big

Dave's secret because she got all excited and her eyes started twinkling (although that could have been the electric-blue eyeliner). And what's more, Nina says she never tells lies. (But actually that's probably a lie in itself, because everyone tells little lies from time to time. I'm always doing it. If Grace asks me if her bum looks big in her skinny jeans, I always say it looks tiny when I know it looks massive. However, if I say it looks massive, she turns into Ninja Grace and this is very bad for me.)

The second clue is Big Dave said *we*, not *I*. It is clear to me that he has a family. A person living on his own would not say *we*.

My third and final clue, and one that can never be hidden, is *Caroline 1973* inked on Big Dave's upper arm. Thanks to Grace leaving her gossip magazines on the living room table, I know that lots of stars get the names of their wives and children tattooed all over their body. And Big Dave can't really deny the evidence when it's written on his skin. (Suddenly, I catch myself wondering if Dad has the name Busty Babs tattooed on his body. Even worse, does he have the name of the beefy boy with the windmill arms too?)

Grace looks a bit surprised when I knock on her bedroom door, offering what's left of the popcorn and asking if she wants in on Operation Reichenbach.

"Right 'n' Back? It sounds like some American football team," she says.

When I explain my mission, Ninja Grace nods her head and tells me it's about time we joined forces to flush out the traitor in our midst. I try to say that this is investigative and not a witch hunt, but she says Big Dave is guilty until proven innocent. With her next breath, Grace says she wants to do something so utterly crazy that I'm speechless. That's when she takes the opportunity to gulp down all the remaining popcorn. "You'll come round to my way of thinking," she says, wiping bits of popcorn from her lips. "You mark my words."

But you can't really. Mark words, that is. And no way is what she suggested ever going to happen, I think, as I'm in the bathroom swabbing the inside of my cheek with a cotton bud an hour later. What Grace suggested was stark raving bonkers on the madness scale. We'd be caught for sure, and that's if I could even find out Big Dave's address. I can't get the directory out again when it took me an hour to clean up the hallway last time.

The cotton bud looks a bit slimy when I pull it from my mouth. I think there's a bit of popcorn on it. You never see that happening on the TV. On the telly, when they take a swab for DNA, they never end up with chunks of someone's movie-time treat.

I had planned to put the cotton bud into a little plastic bag and keep it safe, because you never know when your DNA might be needed to prove that your dad is a big telly star. But what if there was a court case and I had to present this one as evidence:

Prosecution: M'lud. This boy's DNA does not match Malcolm Maynard's DNA.

Defence: Objection! I think you'll find we are one hundred per cent certain it does. This is his son.

Prosecution: This swab only proves that the boy is half toffee-popcorn.

Defence: We think when you chew over the facts you will see we are correct.

I laugh and throw the popcorn-covered bud towards the bathroom bin. It misses and I sigh, then try to pick it up with my bare toes rather than my hands. When that doesn't work I bend down and grab it and set it inside the bin beside an empty packet. Something makes me pull the packet out of the bin.

It's a pregnancy testing kit.

CHAPTER 9

Although Grace's belly is rounded it doesn't look much different than it did before. The stupid baggy T-shirt with purple graffiti that says Good girls are heavenly but bad girls are devilishly good doesn't help much.

"What are you gawping at?" Grace hisses, easing her body across the sofa like a lazy starfish. "If it's my breasts I'm telling Mum." There goes number two on my list. I can't ask for a new sister who doesn't say horrible things if the old one is pregnant and needs my help.

I have to think fast. "I was reading your slogan."

"Oh, that," she says, pulling the T-shirt flat and looking down. "Pretty cool, *non*?"

Non! It is not pretty cool and speaking in French isn't going to change the fact that my sister is pregnant. As my eyes linger on her stomach, Grace folds an arm across her middle, covering my view, and with her other hand she picks up the remote control and flicks channels.

"Look who it isn't." Grace groans. "We cannot escape this man."

Up pops Dad, chatting about a traffic situation to the west of the Paradise estate. He says we should avoid the MacNab roundabout, where there has been an unfortunate collision, and we should also steer clear of the Milton underpass. Beneath his glasses I can see violet crescent-moons, and a small tuft of silver hair juts out from above his left ear. Occasionally his hand strays across the wild expanses of the Sahara desk. Then it moves back again and he clears his throat.

"Why make him your hero?" says Ninja Grace. "He's nobody."

I shake my head. "He's a star, look at him."

"We don't want a star. We want a dad."

Sometimes it's impossible to answer Ninja Grace back because she's always got a smarter response to the genius reply that took you ages to think up.

But the real problem is, Grace has a point. Although it's amazing seeing your dad on the TV, I've come to the conclusion that I would like him to do normal things again, like pick me up from school and play football in Paradise Parade.

Dad shakes his head and gives us a smile that's so wide there could be a watermelon slice jammed in his mouth. He says he'd like to introduce us to a stunning weather girl – as if he's seen a whole parade of weather girls and this one was the best. "She's so beautiful," he says, "that I married her." Grace and I look at each other, horrified. "Drum roll, please." There isn't an actual drum roll, but my heart is doing a good impression. "Welcome to Barbara Ann Maynard." The camera cuts away to a woman standing in front of a weather map.

My eyeballs bulge like they're bursting out of a super squishy mesh ball. Busty Babs is dressed as a beautiful ladybird, in a red and black polka-dot dress. It's so clingy you can tell what she's eaten for lunch (apparently nothing more than a grape). Sheets of blonde hair cascade to her shoulders and she breaks into an easy smile, displaying teeth that could be mistaken for a string of creamy pearls.

"Eau de vinegar," snaps Grace. "I don't know what he ever saw in her."

I could take a wild guess.

"She's not how I imagined," I say softly.

"She'd better not be," Grace says, squinting at me. Grace proceeds to tell me she hates nepotism, which is apparently something to do with getting your friends and family into a job. Well, that's a lie for a start, because she follows it up with, "If we were still friendly with Dad and there was a fabulous job going as a weather girl, then I should have got it."

"Don't you have to get your GCSEs first?" I ask.

"Pffttt…" Grace glares at me. "Who cares? I've already got a degree in common sense."

"At least you'd know you hadn't got it for your looks," I admit. But Ninja Grace bares her teeth and I have to hastily retreat. "You'd get it because you're so clever, I mean."

"Ain't that the truth," replies Grace, "and because I'm smart, I'm switching over."

I clear my throat and ask if we're going to have to skip the weather report from now on. "We'll not know if it's raining or sunny," I say glumly.

"Look out the window," Grace says.

Life has a habit of biting you in the bum, that's what Mum says. Well, she doesn't actually say "bum", but that's another story. Just when I think there's no unbitten bits left on my bottom, Mrs Parfitt takes another chunk of flesh when she tells us our next task on Project Eco Everywhere is to do a hero show-and-tell. Is there no end to this Project Eco Everywhere misery? Apparently, we've got to bring in an item our hero has given us and talk to the class about it for one minute. Sixty whole seconds of suffering.

I'm panicking about what item I'm going to be able to bring in. Dad didn't give me much. All I can think of is the teddy bear he bought me at the beach. I was only six years old and I got lost. Fear nibbled at my insides, I remember that much, and I thought I'd never see Dad again. I ran around in circles, searching everyone's face, desperate to find him. When there was no sign, I went back to where I started and lay curled up on the sand, sobbing as if the world had ended. Water lapped up the beach and I thought I'd build a giant sandcastle and crawl inside, and then wait until the sea carried me away. But Dad found me, bought me a teddy bear and wiped away my sandy tears with its paws. Dad said the teddy should be called Destiny, because it was destiny that we'd never be parted, that he'd always find me, no matter how far I'd wandered away from him. But this time it isn't me who has wandered.

"I'm going to bring in my new calculator," whispers Kevin Cummings. "Dad says I need to use it if I'm to work out my tax situation. He says I must always know how much I'm owed."

"I'm bringing in a cross that touched the hand of someone who touched the hair of someone who kissed the statue of the Virgin Mary at a replica of the grotto in Lourdes. Mum bought the cross for me because she said the Virgin Mary knows a lot about obedience and I could learn a few lessons from her," announces Jo. "What about you, Christopher?"

Christopher goes red and says, "I thought about bringing in Boo because Dad bought him for me, but the school said health and safety wouldn't allow me to bring in a hamster." Christopher looks at me and I know it's my signal to tell him what I'm bringing in.

My mouth drains of saliva. Nowhere in my mind do I want to admit I'm bringing in a bear with one button for an eye and a paw covered in salty tear stains. Perhaps I should bring in the planet mobile from Big Dave and pretend it was from my dad. At least it wouldn't be embarrassing, but then again it's sort of cheating.

"I bet Dan will have something really good," says Jo, twisting her hair into a knot and shoving a pencil in it.

Christopher looks at her and then looks at me as I nod and mouth the word "Yeah". I like Jo's confidence, but it's completely misguided. Jo leans across the desks and whispers into my ear, asking me if Saint Gabriel of Our Lady of Sorrows is healing me. I shake my head and catch Christopher's eye. And then I wish I hadn't, because he's trying to knock me out using the power of his pupils alone. There's no question about it, Christopher likes Jo Bister, but for some strange reason he's convinced I like her too. I do, but not in the way he thinks. I mean, we're just mates, nothing more. I move away from Jo and say very loudly, "Thanks, Jo, but I'll let you know when I get the time."

That's when Mrs Parfitt tells us all to be quiet and listen up because she wants us to bring in our hero items tomorrow. "And I don't want any half-baked stories." She continues, "I want to feel the passion you have for your hero. Remember, this is the person you look up to. I expect you to have plenty to say, you normally do. As I mentioned before, it would be lovely is your hero was a member of your family. However…" She pauses. "If it isn't, it should be someone special, a person you look up to. Like a teacher, perhaps."

Kevin Cummings chokes and then disguises it with a huge sneeze, which he says is thanks to his allergies.

"Are you allergic to work?" replies Mrs Parfitt, giving him The Look. The Look means: *You know you're lying and I know you're lying but I'm not going to waste my breath discussing it.* "Anyway, moving on swiftly," says Mrs Parfitt. "This is your homework. You'll present it tomorrow." No one is listening because the home bell has gone and we're all gathering up our belongings and vaulting chairs to get to the door first.

I thought I moved fast but Jo moves faster. She blocks my exit and asks me if I wrote a list of ten things for Saint Gabriel. Again, Jo insists it will work. From where I'm standing, I can feel the heat of a fireball whooshing up Christopher's cheeks. He pushes past us and says he has an important appointment with friends who don't exclude him.

As I squeeze past Jo and rush after Christopher, she shouts, "Stop running away from things. Saint Gabriel is looking out for you."

"Hey, wait up, Christopher!" I say, trying to sound forceful.

The force isn't with me, because Christopher keeps walking.

"Jo isn't my girlfriend," I tell him as we reach the school playground. My whole body has turned into a worm, wriggling and squirming with embarrassment. "What I'm trying to say is, we're just *friends*." My footsteps follow the rhythm of his. "We were talking about a medal."

"What sort of medal?" Christopher doesn't look at me but quickens his pace.

"It's not important," I call as Christopher runs away and disappears out through the school gates, passing Grace and Stan. "Well, it isn't!" I shout, concentrating on looking as though I'm not bothered that he's run away.

"He's in a hurry," says Grace, doing a double-take.

Now, here's the thing. I think you can tell a lot from body language. Like if you're angry you put your hands in a fist, and if you're telling lies you keep touching your nose. Well, this is the first time I've seen Stan since I found Grace's pregnancy test and in body language terms, his face is pretty much channelling new-father-to-be-with-added-super-turbo-bits.

"Hey, Squirt," Stan says, lounging against the wall.

"My name isn't Squirt."

He sighs, as if I am a squirt but not old enough to know it, then says, "Okay, I won't call you Squirt again. Is Big Man any better?"

"Suits me," I say, making it sound as though it doesn't.

Our banter is obviously boring Grace because she launches into a heavy conversation about what university Stan should apply to. Stan twiddles his cobweb 'tache and says he knows a uni with the best fresher week. Grace gives a tinkling laugh that sounds totally false and I look at her, slack-jawed. How can she possibly make plans about university when she's having a baby?

"You don't have to buy expensive drinks at the bar. You can bring a bottle," says Stan, throwing his arm around her shoulder.

"Yeah, of milk," I whisper to myself.

Instead of taking ten minutes, the walk home drags on for ever. Grace and Stan are busy holding 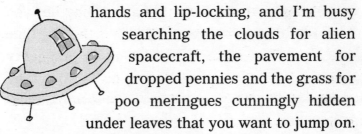 hands and lip-locking, and I'm busy searching the clouds for alien spacecraft, the pavement for dropped pennies and the grass for poo meringues cunningly hidden under leaves that you want to jump on. Anything that means I do not have to watch them kissing and pawing each other.

When Stan leaves us at the fork in the road, Grace makes him a heart with her thumbs and index fingers. Then she turns to me and says, "Now he's gone we need to have a little chat. Remember Operation Right 'n' Back?"

"Reichenbach," I correct her.

"Yeah, that. The time has come to see what Big Dave's little game is."

My face freezes. I didn't like Grace's idea the first time she mentioned it and I don't like it any better now. "Isn't it a bit risky?" I want to follow that up with "in your condition", but I don't. However, when I get a chance I'm going to look up pregnancy on the internet, because it's obvious to me that Ninja Grace has gone completely potty with a capital P.

"Not the way I'm going to do it," Grace assures me. "All you have to do is await my instructions and then I guarantee we'll know a lot more about *Caroline 1973*. More than Big Dave wants us to. Grace Hope is ready. Right 'n' Back has begun."

I wish I'd never started this.

CHAPTER 10

Christopher is waiting for me at the school gates with two henchmen by his side. One is class comedian Kevin Cummings, who has his finger so far up his nose that he could pick his own brains, and the other is Dirk from the year below. Dirk, also commonly known as Dork, is picking a whitehead and seems mightily impressed when it releases a jet of pus lava.

"Great, I wanted to talk to you about yesterday," I say to Christopher, ignoring the other two. "It's about Jo. I think you've got things mixed up."

Dork, meanwhile, is mopping up the pus with

the cuff of his white shirt and Kevin has removed his finger from his nose and is staring at the tip of it as though he's unearthed a prize emerald. Neither of them is paying any attention when Christopher grabs my school bag and shot-puts it over the hedge.

"Nope, *you're* mixed up," whispers Christopher. "I never said I liked Jo."

That proves it! I didn't say a thing about Christopher liking Jo. All I said was that I thought he might have got things mixed up. I give a tiny smile, which is my biggest mistake ever, because Christopher flips his lid and grabs me by my hand and spins me round like I'm a washing machine. Without warning, Christopher releases his grip.

5...4...3...2...1...
Lift-off!
Daniel Hope is a rocket. ☆

When the school bell goes off, Christopher peers at me lying on my landing pad in the hedge, picks up my school bag and wanders off whistling, like he hasn't a care in the world. I, on the other hand, am blowing on my fingers like billy-o and blinking because there is something in my eye.

My confusion follows me into the classroom, where Christopher is ignoring me and my school bag has been returned to my desk. Occasionally I try to look in his direction, but he stares through me as though I'm the ghost of the Invisible Man. Perhaps I underestimated how much Christopher likes Jo. I'll try to make it up to him and I'll never mention that Christopher likes Jo in front of Kevin Cummings again. That could be where I went wrong this morning.

"So," Mrs Parfitt says, "let's get straight on with your homework. You were asked to bring in an item connected with your hero and talk about it. First up..." Mrs Parfitt moves between the desks, her blouse billowing like the sail on a galleon. "Christopher. Stand up."

Christopher pushes out his chair and takes a watch from his pocket and holds it up for the whole class to look at. The floor is his. Christopher proceeds to tell us that his dad bought him this watch. Then he launches into a fabulous speech about how it symbolizes their life with the passing of time. "If you look closely," he says, "there is a small dial that shows the sun through the day and the stars at night."

Everyone oohs and ahhs, except Kevin Cummings, who ums and fidgets. Mrs Parfitt takes the watch and studies it, then passes it around the desks. When it reaches me I roll it around in my hand, then stare at the small sun in the dial, wishing my dad had bought me something so ace. My foot knocks against my school bag and I swallow when I think about bringing out Destiny.

Last night I got into a complete flap trying to think of an item for the presentation. In the end I decided I'd bring in the planet mobile. Exhausted, I fell asleep. But when I woke up this morning, the last few planets had fallen off the mobile and Charles Scallybones had eaten them. All I was left with was string and a small pile of sick. So I threw the bear in my rucksack and prayed that the moment to talk about it wouldn't come.

As Christopher cruises towards the big finale, I hold my breath. "Dad says I mean the world to him." *Boom boom tish!* Christopher hits invisible cymbals, stealing the entire show. An easy grin spreads over his face as the class erupts into applause. "Follow that," he mouths, looking directly at me.

"Well, that was very special indeed," says Mrs

Parfitt. "Thank you, Christopher. Next up..." I slink down in my chair and pretend to study my pen. Ballpoint pens are very fascinating. I read somewhere that on average one hundred people a year choke on ballpoints and that you can write for up to five miles before the ink runs out.

"Daniel. On your feet." Mrs Parfitt was not fooled by my ballpoint-love distraction technique. What I should have done is tried the stare-straight-at-the-teacher technique, in the hopes she would choose someone else. Mind you, that can fail too, because if you look straight at Mrs Parfitt she sometimes picks you anyway. (The moral of this story is that you cannot second-guess a teacher.)

My cheeks flame as I set my school bag on the desk and rummage inside for Destiny. I'm still fumbling about twenty seconds later as Mrs Parfitt taps her toe against the table leg.

Exasperated, she lets out this long sigh.

I look up at her with puppy dog eyes and say, "It's gone."

"Uh-huh." Mrs Parfitt's toe taps quicker as she prepares to give me The Look. "Did you bring it in? Are you looking properly?"

Of course I'm looking properly. I could put on a pair of magnifying glasses but the bear still wouldn't be there. A small stifled giggle takes me by surprise and I fire round to see who is laughing. Christopher forces his hand over his mouth and then makes a big deal of pretending his sides aren't splitting. He did it – of course he did. When he grabbed my school bag earlier he must have stolen my teddy bear. I give him my best glare, only he doesn't notice because he's too busy staring at the bookcase at the front of the classroom. Everyone else stares too and Saleem points his finger and laughs. Sometimes your body has a sense of impending doom and that's what I feel as I turn in slow motion to face the bookcase. There, nestled between the books, is Destiny with a pitta in his tear-stained paw.

"Look, it's a teddy bear's picnic!" shouts Christopher.

I want him to shut up. I want to hurt him. "My mum bought me that bear," I say, lying. "But what would you care? You don't have a mum." As soon as the words blunder from my lips I feel guilt, sharp as the crease on a new pair of school trousers. Christopher's face crumples and he jumps up from his seat and grabs me by my V-neck as Mrs Parfitt shouts at us to stop.

Christopher lets go of me but not before he whispers, "You're going to get it, Dan Hope. Watch your back. You won't know where or when. Didn't you see me in that tae kwon do class? I've got a class tonight and I'm deadly. I could kill you with this." He crooks his little finger, puffs out his anger and sits back down.

Mrs Parfitt lifts my teddy bear from the bookcase. "No harm done," she says, dusting him off and handing him back to me. "Let's just say it was a silly prank and one that won't ever happen again." Mrs Parfitt looks pointedly at Christopher, who is shaking his head. "I think Christopher is sorry so let's continue with our show-and-tell. I want to hear all about this lovely teddy bear who likes eating pitta bread."

Obviously, I get through it and the class claps politely and Mrs Parfitt puts a gold star by my name on the whiteboard. All I can think is: *I don't deserve a star for my bear story.* To be honest, it's a pity star.

Later that afternoon, when I find an envelope in my pocket, I think it must be an apology from Christopher. I carry it to the only private reading place in the whole school: the toilet cubicle. As I lock the door and peel open the envelope, a person enters the urinals. They shuffle about, unzip their flies, grunt, and then I hear the release of water.

"No way," I yell as I start reading the letter.

A voice squeaks, "I've soaked my shoes." I hear the rasp of a zip and the squelch of footsteps as they leave the urinals.

"No way," I repeat. "I don't want to do this." I fold up the letter and stick it back in my pocket.

At three forty-five, Grace arrives at the school gates. Her nose and mouth are the only things visible beneath her furry-hooded coat. "You got my letter then," she says, blowing warmth into her fingers.

I think about it for a nanosecond before saying, "We'll get caught. That's if we can even find out where Big Dave lives."

"Oh yes," replies Grace. "I forgot to mention that I've already done a little digging and know where he lives."

"What?"

"After he left our house I accidentally found myself walking behind him until he went into this house on the Ireland estate."

"Whoa! You followed Big Dave and staked out his house. That's so wrong." I stop, remembering how I was hiding in Dad's garden only a few nights ago.

"Get off your high horse. It must be cold up there," says Grace, her eyes like flint. "I did it for Mum, remember." That's Grace's answer to everything, because if she says she's doing it for Mum then I can't exactly argue. She hands me a balaclava and a toy walkie-talkie. "We need to be in disguise and in communication at all times."

"Where did you find the walkie-talkies?"

"Under your bed," Grace replies. "I had to wear rubber gloves, mind. Didn't want to touch that pants graveyard you've got under there."

I stick the woolly balaclava over my head and sigh into the wool. This day is turning into an epic disaster, so I might as well hide my shame behind a knitted sheep.

When we reach Big Dave's house we separate. Grace directs me to a bush on the opposite side of the road and she takes the easier hiding place behind Big Dave's car. I click on the walkie-talkie. "This balaclava is making me sweat, over," I mumble.

Grace clicks her walkie-talkie on. "Stop bleating or we'll alert the neighbours, over."

"You don't think a stranger lurking in a holly bush will do that? Over."

"Not if you crouch down and stop complaining, over."

"Easy for you to say when you don't have a piece of holly up your bum. Why did you bring these walkie-talkies when we could have communicated via mobile phones? Over." My eyes peep through the holes in the balaclava.

"Duck, over," hisses Grace, diving down. "Neighbour twitching curtains but trying to pretend they're adjusting fairy lights on Christmas tree."

"Over, over," I mutter into the walkie-talkie.

"Over what?"

"You forgot to say over, over," I say, breaking cover. When I run across the road and join Ninja Grace, she aims the walkie-talkie at my ear hole. "But saying over is um...overrated anyway," I say.

"Let's just stick to the plan and quit with the smart comments," replies Grace, putting the walkie-talkies in her bag. "We're supposed to be staking the place out to see if he's there or not and if there's any sign of *Caroline 1973*. After that we can make a decision on what to do next."

Big Dave's doorbell parps when I push it and Grace is hiding in next door's garden. The door flings open and Big Dave stands in front of me, looking baffled. "Hello?"

"Hello," I mutter through a mouthful of wool, wishing that Grace's plan of staking the place out didn't actually involve me ringing the bell.

"Hallowe'en is in October not December." Big Dave shakes his head and starts to close the door until I shove my foot in it.

"Ta-da. It's me." I pull the balaclava up so Big Dave can see my face.

"Arrggh," he says. "Put the mask back on, it's an improvement."

I have to think fast to explain why I'm on Big Dave's doorstep in a balaclava. Unfortunately, my brain is thinking so fast that my mouth doesn't catch up and I say, "Umm...I was taking Charles Scallybones for a walk and I spotted your car. The tyres are flat." I fold my arms and try to look concerned and even stroke my chin, which is a sure sign I'm perplexed by this matter. "I thought you'd like to know, so that's why I rang the bell."

"Where?" Big Dave asks.

"Where are the car tyres?" I look at him as though he's stupid and point to his silver Mondeo parked outside the house.

"No, where is the dog?"

I say the first thing that comes into my head. That first thing being a load of utter drivel. "Chasing rabbits. This housing estate is riddled with them." Big Dave looks at me and pulls a face but follows me to the Mondeo anyway.

For the next five minutes I try to explain to Big Dave why the tyres look flat. Unfortunately, I am no match for the car mechanic that is Big Dave who is now explaining, without drawing breath, that he checked them yesterday when they were a perfect 32psi and they don't look any different.

"Let me sit in it," I say, stalling for time. "I want to learn to drive."

"You're eleven."

"Yes and you're about forty and it doesn't stop you. I've read the driving theory book cover to cover," I say. "And it's never too early to sit in such a fabulous car and get a feel for it. You know that I love your Mondeo." Out of the corner of my eye I see Grace actually exit from Big Dave's house with something pink draped over her arms. She must have sneaked in when I was talking. My stomach catapults as she bounds into the neighbour's garden and drops behind the hedge and out of sight once more.

"If you love it so much, I suppose I could get the car keys," says Big Dave, looking at me.

"Nah, you're alright," I say, walking away. "I don't love it as much as I did five minutes ago."

Grace catches me up at the alleyway beside The Frying Squad. She looks triumphant and in her hand she's holding a pink silk dressing gown. "You're not going to believe this," she says.

From the look on her face, I'm guessing she's right.

CHAPTER 11

New information received today via the internet: Unborn babies look like aliens.

Pregnancy is also known as: *The Club*.

Notes about *The Club*: Boys can't join. I do not care because *The Club* does not seem like fun. If you are a member you must be ratty with everyone. You will act strangely from time to time. This is your hormones. (Hormones explain why Grace did something so crazy at Big Dave's house.)

New members must: Smell like a dog. Not literally. But your nose will be like a bloodhound's muzzle and will pick up strange scents that make you sick.

Sick: As in puke, not as in good.

Length of membership: Life. What's more, you will never be allowed to jump on a trampoline any more in case you wet yourself.

You will be in stitches: Apparently, while in stitches you won't want to laugh. Confused? I know I am.

Worries: *The Club*. Grace is no good with stuff like this. She couldn't even stick it out for a month at Brownies.

Important: Take folic acid.

From what I'm reading, Grace's pregnancy is doomed – doomed, I tell you. I click on another page and scroll down until I find a clip of a tadpole and his buddies swimming towards a full moon. This is like a big tadpole party. Unlike a human party, they all want to get there first. In real life, turning up first is for losers. One tadpole dies, actually conks out in front of his mates, and they swim on totally unconcerned. No tadpole funeral for him, by the looks of it. They're harsh, these tadpoles. Eventually, one little tadpole reaches the full moon and almost does a fist punch, if he had any fists. I figure that I need to get Grace this folic acid stuff, because if she doesn't take it she might end up giving birth to a frog.

Underneath the tadpole party there is a stick drawing of a man and woman. The man has a full fluffy beard, nothing like Stan, and the woman is smuggling a football under her puffy dress. She looks nothing like Grace either. Grace only has one puffy dress and she wore it to her first Communion, with a veil. The stick lady isn't wearing a veil. Apparently, veils have nothing to do with *The Club*.

I ease back into my seat and scratch my head. So a lot of the information I've found suggests that pregnant people act weird. Which in turn explains Grace's act of stupidity last night. It's all because she's in *The Club* and there are tadpoles having a party in her belly.

After we'd been to Big Dave's house Grace told me she'd found all the evidence of *Caroline 1973* that she needed. "The bedroom was ready for love and lit with scented candles," she said. "Sandalwood, I think."

"Are you sure?" I asked.

"Not about the sandalwood," she replied. "Could have been amber, I suppose. But I'm quite sure it was a love nest. And I nearly got caught. Someone went to the toilet while I was in the bedroom and I had to grab the first thing I could and run. I knocked over some stuff on the dressing table, including a bottle of Poison."

"Poison?"

To my horror, Grace laughed. Then she said, "Poison is a perfume, you idiot. We won't tell Mum about this yet but we're *definitely* going to tell her when the time is right."

"Who decides when the time is right?"

"Me." Grace rubbed her hands together like a pantomime villain.

"Why are you drawing boobs?" asks Kevin Cummings.

"They're not. They're footballs with spots in the centre," I reply. Kevin is not convinced and says as much. "Okay, they're boobs," I admit, hoping this is the end of the matter. No such luck because when I say I don't want to talk about it, Kevin Cummings sticks up his hand.

"Mrs Parfitt, guess what?" he whines.

As she approaches I have to draw smiley faces on the boobs and hiss to Kevin that I'll tell him the whole story later. Grinning, Kevin tells Mrs Parfitt he needs the toilet. As he slips out of the classroom he pulls the front of his school jumper out to make it look like he's got moobs (which he does anyway).

This is the point where I come unstuck. I plan to run away after school, but Kevin Cummings is too clever for me. Just before the bell rings he tells Mrs

Parfitt his bowels have gone into meltdown thanks to a right royal disaster, otherwise known as The King Kebab with extra jalapeño sauce. Since there's an inferno in his guts, could he possibly go to the toilet again, take his school bag and then go home from there? When her back is turned he makes his armpit fart and suddenly she can't wait to let him go. Only, Kevin Cummings has no intention of getting up to his knees in toilet paper – instead he's waiting at the school gate for me.

"What's with the boobs?" asks Kevin as we walk away from school.

"What's with your guts?" Kevin has a habit of answering a question with a question, which is annoying, so I've learned to use his own trick against him.

"You got a girlfriend?" he asks.

The easiest and quickest answer to get him off my back is yes. When I take this option he replies, "Nah, you don't."

"Okay, promise you won't tell?"

"Cross-my-heart-and-hope-to-die."

"Grace is in *The Club*," I say.

"What club?" Kevin looks at me blankly. When I wink at him and tell him it's *The Club*, he makes an onion ring of his mouth. "Oh, I get you now. Who's the father?"

That's when I make a big mistake – bigger than the big mistake of telling him in the first place. "It's Stan," I say as I cross the road. "But you can't tell anyone."

"Wow. That streak of bacon. I'm impressed." Then Kevin says something I'm not too happy about. "By the way, I crossed my fingers when I promised not to tell." Everyone knows that crossing your fingers cancels out a cross-my-heart-and-hope-to-die.

I wonder if a punch to the guts cancels out a crossing your fingers.

"Okay, so now I've told you my secret, you can do something for me," I say, narrowing my eyes. Kevin looks confused as I explain that I need him to go into the chemist to get some acid for Mum's car battery. "It's called folic acid," I say.

"Why can't you do it yourself?"

I pull my mobile phone from my school bag and switch it back on. We're allowed to take phones into school but not switch them on, so this is the first chance I've had to use it all day. "It's the baby. I've got to make an urgent call to Grace. Here's some money."

"Oh," says Kevin and he takes the cash. "I suppose it'll only take a minute." He nips into the small chemist at the end of the road while I wait outside, mouthing into the phone.

On his return, Kevin hands me a small bag. He looks ill and is sweating like cheese left out on a hot day. "What did Grace say?"

"Nothing," I reply. "I forgot to ring her."

Kevin leans against the wall and wipes his forehead on the arm of his blazer jacket. "I asked the chemist for folic acid to rev up an engine. Then the chemist said my engine was in fine working order if it was folic acid I was after." He glares and his jaw hardens. "After that, he asked how old I was. 'Excuse me,' I said, 'but what has my age got to do with it?' The chemist burst out laughing, as did a queue of old ladies. It was so hilarious the ladies had to cross their legs and the chemist directed them to pads."

"Brake pads," I say, trying not to laugh.

"I know what sort of pads they were," says Kevin. "My nan is always buying them." Kevin storms off (as much as you can storm off when the strap on your school bag snaps).

The folic acid tablets don't look too scary. They're small and white, a bit like the circle of paper that comes out of a mini hole-punch. I stare at the bottle as I walk home and it's still in my hand when I step into the house – which is a mistake, because Mum is in the hallway. "What's that you've got?" asks Mum and – abracadabra! – I have to pull off this fantastic magic trick that makes the folic acid disappear down the back of my trousers.

"Nothing," I reply, clenching my bottom to stop them falling down my leg.

"Oh, right." Mum starts going on about her dysfunctional digestive system. "Honestly, I've not known whether I'm up or down in that toilet bowl. But there's an end in sight." She rubs her nose. "I just can't quite see it among the diced carrots."

"You were ill last week too," I reply, squeezing my bum cheeks together. "It must be what you're bringing home from Aladdin's."

Mum laughs. "I can assure you that there's nothing wrong with what I'm bringing home. You're eating it, aren't you?"

So I say, "You're not dying, and keeping it a secret from me, are you?" And *clench*.

After that, Mum says she *is* dying but then so is everyone else from the moment they're born. That's the best explanation she can offer. Anyway, she says she has no plans to die quite yet and it's nothing I need to worry about.

"That's okay then," I say. "I can't lose you." The bottle feels like it's slipping until I do another quick bum squeeze.

Mum smiles and nudges my arm. "Stop standing in the hallway fretting about things that aren't going to happen. I can assure you this is nothing whatsoever to do with me dying. We can't be parted, Dan Hope."

I can't move and it's nothing to do with the folic acid hidden in my trousers. It's because a little part of me can't help remembering that that's what Dad said once.

CHAPTER 12

On Tuesday I try to give Jo the medal back. Instead of Saint Gabriel helping me, he's making everything go wrong. I've got hardly anything left on my list and I don't believe he's going to make a dream come true. I tell her I wasn't unhappy to begin with so I don't need to hold onto him. I urge her to give him to some other poor person who is truly sad and needs healing.

"That is the precise reason why you need it. You're still sad and need healing," echoes Jo, pressing Saint Gabriel of Our Lady of Sorrows back into my palm. She holds my hand for a second.

"Keep it. I won't accept it back. I know you're not going to tell me what's going on but I want you to understand that Saint Gabriel is here for you." She nods knowingly. "Remember how he sent me a feather. It was a sign from beyond the grave. That's what I wanted most and it happened to me because I believed."

From the corner of my eye I can see Christopher staring at us and I pull away from Jo's grip. Too late – Christopher's turned away. "Hallelujah, Jo," I say firmly, "but I don't need you to tell me how to feel. And I've told you before where I think feathers come from." As I force the medal back into my pocket I cannot get the image of a bird's bum out of my mind. Jo looks upset and walks away, but not before telling me she knows I'm hurting, so she'll try to forgive me.

"Just so you know, there were no birds around when Grandma sent me that feather," Jo calls back. "And by the way, you need to brush your teeth in holy water because the words coming from your mouth are cruel."

Is it cruel not to believe in a bit of metal? Is it cruel to be angry that my friend Christopher has deserted me because of it? Is it cruel that nothing on my stupid list has come true? And am I losing my marbles by asking myself all these stupid questions about whether things are cruel? I had to score off the new bike (number five) when Mum said she was buying me something small for Christmas. And I gave up on number three when Charles Scallybones brought up another pirate, a rowing boat, a skeleton and the Southern hemisphere (aka the bottom half of my planet mobile).

Jo turns back and looks at me again as I stand like a broken robot in the middle of the busy playground. When I pull a face at her, she lifts her nose in the air and marches off to the girls' toilets. At that point Kevin trots over and gives me a sympathy punch on my arm. And I give him a sympathy punch to the stomach and say, "Can't you see I'm busy?"

"Busy being a no-mates," replies Kevin. "Jo didn't look too happy with you."

"She'll get over it."

Kevin shrugs. "I hope you'll get over this. After I left you yesterday I bumped into Stan. I may have congratulated him on being a father." Kevin ducks, which is probably not a bad idea as my fist appears to have shot out to grab his jumper. "I did cross my fingers, which means I didn't have to keep it a secret

– I told you." His voice rises so high my ears are bleeding.

"You're joking," I say, curling my hand into a fist. "This is payback for the folic acid, isn't it?"

"I'm not joking," Kevin replies, retreating into his jumper. "I really did cross my fingers."

The toilet block wall is very hard, as I discover by banging my head off it a few times. "This isn't happening to me."

Kevin whispers, "It is."

Thanks to Foghorn Cummings, the apocalypse is nigh. So the rest of the afternoon, while Mrs Parfitt is talking about Project Eco Everywhere, I'm writing my will under the desk.

I, Daniel George Hope, bequeath my dog, Charles Scallybones the First, to Aunty Pat. Mum says Aunty Pat's only friend is the bottle. Now she can have a new friend. What's more, Aunty Pat has loads of ornaments which Charles Scallybones could eat and sick back up. This would be a fitting end for her pottery.

I bequeath my A–Z book of medical problems to my mother. If, for some reason, Mum dies before me, I wish the book to go to Grace and she should turn to page 122 for information on what to do when one boob is much bigger than the other.

I bequeath my membership to the local soft play area to Grace. Of course, I realize she may not have any interest in rolling around in a ball pit, but at least she can cancel this membership, unlike The Club, where membership is for life.

I bequeath the Saint Gabriel of Our Lady of Sorrows medal to Kevin Cummings. When he's finished with it he can return it to Jo Bister. Meanwhile, the medal is likely to send him gaga before it ever heals his problems.

Signed: Daniel George Hope, Esq.

As I finish with a flourish, I hear Mrs Parfitt saying, "I hope you're all going to ask your heroes to attend the show." She looks over at Jo. "Perhaps the Virgin Mary won't be able to come but I'm sure she'll be there in spirit."

My heart, which was already at the bottom of an ocean, sinks down to the earth's core. What are the chances of Dad wanting to come? A piece of folded-up paper whizzes in my direction and I open it up and mouth the words: *After school, I've got a surprise for you. Be there or be a chicken.* Christopher catches my eye, nods, then waggles his fingers.

At a guess, this is the sort of surprise that comes wrapped up in a tae kwon do master killing me with his little finger. I quickly look away, but Christopher fires a paper aeroplane. This time I let it sail past me and land on the floor. When he launches another, Mrs Parfitt threatens to make him stand in the corridor if he doesn't stop.

What was it Christopher told me before? I think it was something like "Watch your back". So I cannot leave school today without a plan or I'll be bruised like the peaches Mum brings home from Aladdin's. This is where a bright idea would come in handy. I suppose I could hide in the stationery cupboard until everyone leaves, or I could offer to walk Mrs Parfitt to her car and then follow it into the road and run alongside it until I get far away enough from Christopher to be safe. Or I could just apologize and say I'm completely rubbish.

Completely rubbish! Yee-ha! My bright idea has just touched down.

The Project Eco Everywhere desk is at the back of the classroom and contains all the rubbish everyone brought in to complete their outfits. The things I contributed:

* Two pairs of laddered tights
* An empty bucket of popcorn from Kernel Sanderz
* Microwave chip box – crinkle cut and with sunflower oil
* Toilet roll tubes x 8 and one empty box of diarrhoea relief capsules

The things I think Kevin Cummings contributed:

* Leaflets about self-assessment: because tax isn't taxing

The things I think Jo Bister contributed:

* A plastic statue of Saint Patrick with a broken staff
* A holey holy tea towel
* A piece of burned toast with Jesus' face on it

Although all these items are very interesting, they're no use to me. Luckily there are lots of other things on the table that will help. As Jo is picking up a foil pie case and sniffing it, I edge alongside her and choose a few items for myself. She looks over her shoulder and says her Virgin Mary costume will be nothing short of a miracle, which I agree with, judging by the rubbish she has in her hands. She looks annoyed so I quickly carry my chosen items to my desk, and while no one is looking, put a few bits inside my school bag. Stage one is complete. Stage two finds me and my Project Eco Everywhere items in the boys' toilets after school. First I take off my jumper and school shirt, and then I wind a whole heap of bubble wrap around my belly and replace my shirt and jumper. When I look in the mirror I am a walking advert for who ate all the pies.

Next, as I drop my trousers to my ankles, a Year Three boy comes into the toilets, gives me a weird look and runs out again. Mumbling and sweating, I put half a coconut shell in my pants and yank up my trousers. Then I write I'M NO CHICKEN across my forehead. (It's not easy to write I'M NO CHICKEN using a mirror.)

As I hobble towards the school gate I see Christopher sitting, facing away from me, on the wall. Fury bubbles up in my chest when I think about how he's ruined our friendship over a girl – a girl I don't even fancy. Everything that happens next is a slow-motion scene full of rubbish. I think he hears me coming because he turns around and his jaw drops open. Before he can say a word, I launch myself forward and land on him with a crump. It's like landing on the jelly part of a pork pie. Christopher grabs my belly, which starts popping and exploding, much to his shock. Unfortunately, he's not shocked enough to avoid biffing me. Fortunately, the main part of the biffing includes him bringing his knee up sharply. I feel sure that this type of knee-to-groin move isn't an accepted tae kwon do move. There is a wince of pain in Christopher's eyes when he realizes I'm rock-hard down below.

Next, Christopher rugby-tackles me and as we drop to the ground I feel a furry thing scuttle across my shoulders and into the undergrowth. "Boo!" screams Christopher. "Get back here, you rodent."

"What are you two doing?" Christopher scrabbles to his feet as Grace reaches down and helps me up. "You're going to be in big trouble if Mum finds out you've been fighting. What's it about?"

Christopher says, "I told your lunatic brother I had a surprise and to meet me after school."

"The surprise was to beat me up," I snap.

"No," Christopher says firmly. "If you do tae

kwon do you're not allowed to use it for fighting people at school. Here's the second note you didn't pick up from the floor." He passes me the note and I read it, furious to start with, and then embarrassed.

Dan. Meet me after school. I told you I had a surprise for you. Guess what? It's Boo! He's been living in my pocket all day and no one has even noticed. Didn't you hear him squeak when Mrs Parfitt asked us about the capital of New Zealand?

"Oh," I say. Just *oh*. I tug on Grace's coat sleeve and say it's time we were getting home.

"What are you having for dinner?" shouts Christopher as we walk away. "Humble pie?"

I think he's on his knees calling for Boo, then, but I don't look back. All I can do is limp, putting one painful foot in front of the other. When I can bear it no more, I stop and fish around in my trousers. Grace goes the colour of wet putty and her hands fly in front of her eyes. "Don't worry, I've just been kicked in the coconuts," I say.

"I've heard of it being called many things," replies Grace, peeking through her split fingers, "but not coconuts. Stan would have laughed at that."

I pull an actual coconut shell out of my trousers and say, "It's a long story," before firing it into someone's garden.

Grace's eyebrows shoot into her fringe. "Stan would have liked to hear your long story. And I bet you didn't know that he liked coconuts. Well, he enjoyed a Bounty bar from Biddolpho's Newsagent's, if that counts. Anyway, what does it matter? He dumped me today."

I think it's my turn to go the colour of putty. I reach into my pocket and bring out the will and wave it in front of my face, saying, "Did Stan mention Kevin Cummings from my class?"

"Why would he mention Kevin Cummings?"

The will is quickly brought to my nose and I pretend to give this big blow and then return it to my pocket. From Grace's confusion it's obvious she knows nothing about Kevin Cummings telling Stan she's pregnant. Maybe Stan just broke up with her because she's annoying. To be honest, I often find that the case too.

All the way home she tells me how horrible Stan

is and when I agree with her, she says, "Who asked you? I'm allowed to talk about Stan, but you're not."

When we get back to the house Grace goes straight to her room and doesn't come out for dinner, even though she knows it is potato waffles and she loves those because they've got fewer calories than chips, what with the holes and everything. In fact, Grace stays in her bedroom all evening. Even when I'm upstairs playing guitar, I can hear her wailing through the walls. By the time I've listened to her banshee moans for an hour I can't stand it any longer.

I no u r pregnant. Dan :' (

Six words in my text and they took as much effort as it took Sherlock Holmes to solve all the mysteries in Dad's book. Rather than send my text straight to Grace, I decide I'll give it some more thought and I drop the phone onto the bed before picking up my guitar and letting my fingers slide along the strings. At this point Charles Scallybones jumps on my bed, begins to howl and starts doggy krumping. Now, this would be very funny if I didn't hear a small bleep, the sort of bleep that only comes from sending a text message. I lunge for my mobile but it's too late. Charles Scallybones has sent my text.

The mobile phone might as well be wearing a huge neon sign saying: THE TEXT MESSAGE HAS GONE. AREN'T I BIG AND CLEVER? Yes, my mobile phone is big but it's not clever (it is actually Grace's stupid old phone with glittery girly stickers on it). I half expect Ninja Grace to break through the wall, with her mobile clenched between her teeth and her fist ready to bop me on the head. Nothing happens. Grace is still listening to misery music and every so often there's a muffled sob, but nothing else. Surely Grace would have read it by now?

I scroll down the messages to double-check it's been sent. Yes, it has, but not to Ninja Grace.

CHAPTER 13

I'm no sprinter but I think I just broke the world record for the hundred metres. An Olympic athlete has nothing on Dan Hope when he's trying to get to his mother's mobile phone. As it turns out, my text ended up going to Mum and I need to get to her handbag to stop her receiving it. The bag is in the hallway and I rummage through it as though I'm a trainee surgeon trying to find an appendix. The mobile phone isn't there.

Okay, if it's not there, it's on the coffee table.

Okay, if it's not there, it's in Mum's hand.

Okay, it's *in* Mum's hand. She looks at the display,

furrows her brow and says, "Want a drink?"

"Yah," I reply. What sort of idiot says "Yah"? The sort of idiot who sends their mother a text saying she's pregnant, that's who.

The instant Mum leaves the room I grab the phone and scroll through the messages.

"Orange or milkshake?" Mum pokes her head back into the living room.

The phone goes under my bum as I say, "Squash, please." There is a small vibration as a text comes through. Mum nods and leaves the room again as I pull the phone out from under my bum. This message is from Big Dave:

Sumthin happened a couple of nights ago. Will explain evrything when I ring u l8er. Luv u. By the way when will you break it 2 kids? Hope they understand.

To me, it sounds like there are problems between Big Dave and *Caroline 1973*. It could be that she's discovered the affair and chucked him out. What if he's homeless at Christmas and we have to take him in like a stray mongrel? Surely Mum wouldn't take him in if she knew he had a wife? Underneath Big Dave's message is mine and it has already been read. I quickly put the phone back on the coffee table and run upstairs to hide in the supermassive black hole. Next door, Grace is still listening to misery music and wailing about how she'll never find another man like Stan. Hard to believe: the precinct is full of blokes just like him.

If I had a proper dad none of this would have happened. Jo wouldn't have given me a medal because of my sadness. And if I didn't have the medal, Christopher wouldn't have fallen out with me about my secret chats with Jo. Grace wouldn't have ended up pregnant. Mum wouldn't be dating Big Dave and she wouldn't have got my text. The dog wouldn't have been so sick. (Okay, the dog would still have been sick, but we'd have one extra person to clean it up.) All this mess has happened because Dad isn't here. If Dad came back, we'd be normal again. In fact, our family would be perfect. That's the reason I need to talk to him. If I can make him see sense, everything will come right again.

Downstairs I can hear the phone ringing in the hallway and the slap of Mum's feet as she walks to answer it. There is a click as she picks up the receiver.

After a moment, I hear her say: "How did that even happen?"

Silence.

"That's terrible."

Silence.

"You're lucky to get out alive. Uh-huh... Uh-huh... Uh-huh... Uh-huh."

I hold my breath, waiting for her to say something else.

"Uh-huh."

Forget it, I have to breathe.

"Uh-huh. No, I wouldn't have spent days worrying. You're so lucky it's just a scorch mark on the wallpaper and curtains."

Silence.

"But why were you outside looking at your car tyres? And why leave burning candles unattended in the house? I'm not sure that was a clever thing to do. Your landlord won't be best pleased."

Silence.

"He's what? Given you notice because of some burn marks in the bedroom? That's a bit dramatic of him. Of course it was an accident. Don't worry about it. You've got a home here. I know you didn't want to rush things because Kit wasn't ready, but perhaps this fire is a sign."

Silence.

"Yes, I know you're protecting him."

I stop listening after that. My ears tune out like they do when Mum puts on Radio 2, and all I can hear is a little voice inside my head saying that it's our fault Big Dave's house is charcoal. We're lucky Mum isn't getting a phone call to say he's been flame grilled. Then where would we have been? Ninja Grace could add another name to her list – Ninja Grace Arsonist. That's what they call people who burn things (Kevin told me that when he was experimenting with the sun's rays, a magnifying glass and the school's wooden bench). Grace said she'd knocked stuff over and she'd said there were candles. I bet the candle set fire to the curtains and then *whoosh*, crikey combustibles! Big Dave needs to come live in our house. Where does this leave *Caroline 1973* and their son, Kit? Worse still, if Big Dave moves in with us then there won't be any room for my real dad.

I've got to talk to Dad, and fast.

My opportunity arrives the very next day and it is weird how it happens. Some people might call it fate, but not me. I think it was meant to be. Everything begins with Mrs Parfitt telling the class that she wants to recount a fairy tale.

"Class, my story begins with two fellows. Let us call them Graham and Michael."

Everyone groans. No good story has a main character called Graham.

"Shush." Mrs Parfitt watches us as she glides through the space between the desks. "I think you'll enjoy this tale. Once upon a time Graham and Michael were friends. They played together, they ate together, they chatted and, in fact, they did everything together. One day they fell out with each other. No one knows why. Perhaps it was over a fair maiden: a girl so beautiful and with such long flowing hair that neither could live without her approval. Perhaps it was over who should slay the dragon. Anyway, we know not why and, frankly, it doesn't matter for the purpose of this fairy tale."

The whole class are leaning forward in their seats, hoping the story will go on long enough that we don't have to do our maths test.

"There was a huge fight just beyond the castle turrets: a fight that involved Graham and Michael thumping each other and one of them losing an animal they loved. Let us call this animal Boo. That's a good name for a pet."

My eyes pop when I realize that this story is about me and Christopher. Slowly I try to sink further down in my chair. But Mrs Parfitt isn't finished with us. It's as if she's strapped us into the world's highest drop-tower ride and she's making us do it so many times we feel like puking.

"Someone beautiful and wise had to step in to

save the situation. This lady saw everything from afar. She happened to look outside and saw this unsavoury sight and it made her weep. Anyway, here is what this beautiful and wise woman said: 'Daniel and Christopher, you're living in cloud cuckoo land if you think you're permitted to fight on school premises. For doing so, you will forfeit your rights to something you were looking forward to.' That is what the beautiful and wise woman said."

Everyone in the class turns round to look at me and Christopher. They're nudging and elbowing each other and saying how we're going to live unhappily ever after. A few have their hands over their mouths in case they break out laughing. Kevin is pinching hillocks on his hand to stop himself snorting with glee.

"I think we can drop the whole fairy tale thing now because fighting is not a pretty story. Fighting is ugly and not tolerated. You two will not be allowed onto the stage at the Project Eco Everywhere show. Instead you will be expected to work behind the scenes helping everyone else. Don't think you've been let off lightly, because I haven't finished yet. You will also write fifty lines saying: I AM HAPPY TO WORK WITH MY FRIEND, BEHIND THE SCENES. And..."

Will the agony never end?

"You will not be allowed to do PE this afternoon. Instead you will go to the library and write these lines, and if you have a spare moment, you will think about the misdemeanour. From the library you will go straight home and tomorrow you will come back to school and be the model pupils I know you can be."

Later on, when Mrs Parfitt is going on about prime factorization, I start writing my lines under the desk. By the time I get halfway I've started making mistakes. I AM HAPPY WITH MY BEHIND is the last line I scribble before Mrs Parfitt declares it is time for Christopher and me to take the walk of shame. We're to get our coats and go to the library.

For some reason I take a wrong turning. Easily done. The library is left and I go right and walk straight out the front door and through the school gates. With a whole afternoon free and thoughts of Dad in my mind, I head towards the buildings on the outskirts of town. Luckily, I've got enough bus money and an idea of seeing Dad. This is stage three of Operation Baskerville.

The TV studio looks like a large shard of broken glass nestled between older Victorian buildings. A wintery sun throws a pale wash across the windows and just inside I can see a Christmas tree stretching from floor to ceiling and decorated with hundreds of silver bells. If I go in by the front door I'm going to have to explain why I'm there. And I doubt Dad is going to be impressed if he gets a call from the receptionist saying, "Your son is here."

Sherlock Holmes wouldn't do it that way. He'd use observation. As I wander around the shard, figuring out what I'm going to do next, I spot an open fire exit with stone steps leading up inside the building. The door might as well be saying, *Come in.* This is an open invitation. Checking no one can see me, I slip in and run up the stairs until I come to a door marked *First Floor.* I don't take that one because I'm worried it will be too close to reception. Instead, I run up two more flights. Before I open the door there, I rest my head against the wall. The light from the fluorescent tube above me turns my skin into beige hummus and my breath comes in ragged little gulps.

I'm scared about what I'll find on the other side.

CHAPTER 14

The corridor is littered with photographs of celebrities, including one of Dad and Busty Babs. He has his arms wrapped around her waist and she's staring into his eyes like a pop-eyed colossal squid. Dad looks old and tired but he's wearing a soppy grin and a tie dotted with hearts. I'm staring so hard, I forget I'm standing in a corridor in the TV station building where I'm not supposed to be. Well, I forget until I hear a door open further down and I have to run and turn a corner into another corridor.

The next corridor looks exactly like the one before except there are no photos. It leads to another corridor and another. In the end it's as if I'm in a maze, with no idea how to get back to where I started. Footsteps are coming towards me from an unseen corridor and that's when the panic sets in. I pull open the first door to my right and duck inside. When my eyes adjust to the dimness, I realize I've walked into an empty TV studio. Rows of seats rise diagonally from floor level and there's a stage with two chairs in front of a bright green background.

The temptation to sit in one of the seats is too great. As I settle down, I pretend I'm interviewing Dad.

"So hello, Malcolm Maynard," I say, "or may I call you Dad?"

"Dad would be lovely." I deepen my voice in reply.

"Well, Dad, it's a pleasure to see you again. It's been a long time."

"Has it really?" I raise my eyebrows.

"Four years, five months, fifteen days, fourteen hours, twelve minutes, thirty-six seconds or something like that." I look at my watch to make sure I haven't missed a single moment.

I clear my throat and say gruffly, "I didn't realize. Do you forgive me for not getting in contact sooner?"

Thinking about it for a second, I reply, "I forgive you because you are my dad."

"It will never happen again. From this moment on

we'll be together. We will play football and eat takeaways together. I will come to your school concerts and sports days. I will help you with your homework and teach you to drive. Do you think it will be enough?"

I smile. "It's a start, Dad. And there's one more thing I'd like you to know. You're going to be a granddad."

The invisible audience bursts into imaginary applause and I extend my hand to give Dad's a shake. The breeze brushes my fingers as I lift them up and down.

A head pokes through the door. "Hey, what are you doing in here? We don't allow work experience in the studio. Are you lost?"

"Yes," I say, dropping my hand from the empty handshake. "I'm here for Malcolm Maynard."

The man beckons me over. "Take it from me: you're not going to find him in an empty studio without an audience. Anyway, you're on the wrong floor for work experience. Come with me." He walks off and I follow until we reach a lift. When it opens, the man ushers me inside, saying, "You look very young for work experience. And what's with the school uniform?"

"I had to come straight from school today." The man nods at my answer as if it's entirely logical.

"And um...I'm really sixteen. It's just that I shaved my beard this morning and look baby-faced now." I pull my most grown-up face, which is nothing more than me looking bewildered.

Floor five looks exactly the same as floor three and we work our way through the maze until the man opens a door and tells me to go inside. I stare at the room and then back at him. Dad isn't here, unless he's hiding beneath hundreds of packages and letters. The man tells me this is the post room, where all work experience end up. It seems I'll be opening Malcolm's mail and sorting it into piles. He smiles and leaves me to it.

I pick up a letter addressed to Dad and open it. A fan says how much she is enjoying Malcolm's style of presenting. *You're my only friend. You're in my living room everyday. Could you blow me a kiss?* There is a huge greasy coffee-coloured lipstick stain on the paper.

Letters two, three, four are much the same, only with different shades of lipstick. Letters twenty, twenty-one and twenty-two are asking for autographs. Letters fifty-five, fifty-six and fifty-seven want a photo. Letters sixty-six and sixty-seven are complaining about how Dad looks like he needs a good sleep.

Letter sixty-eight is the one that makes me feel as

though I've swallowed a golf ball. It's from a little girl called Katy and she wants my dad to be her dad because he's much nicer than her own. Apparently, her own dad is always at the pub and never wants to read her stories any more. *If I could have you,* she writes, *all my dad problems would be sorted.*

I squeeze the letter between my fingers and the paper crackles like salt on a frosty path. "You don't want a dad like mine," I say out loud. But I put her letter to the top of the pile, hoping that Dad will reply to her first anyway.

An hour later the door opens and a young woman with four piercings in her left ear and one in her nose appears. "You're the work experience for Malcolm, right?"

I nod rather than speak. That way she can't tell I'm lying.

"If you've sorted out Malcolm's post, you can drop it on his desk if you like."

I nod my head until it almost falls off and she laughs and tells me to follow her to the news floor.

I can hardly wait to see Dad's office and when I do I'm not disappointed. It is a huge open-plan area with loads of people buzzing around and a TV showing the news in the far corner. The lady points to Malcolm's desk and says I am allowed to set the piles of post neatly on top.

This is it! I am in Dad's world. I am so close I can feel the heat from his computer and there is the faint smell of spiced apples – exactly how I remember his aftershave. If I could stand for hours, pour the spiced apples into a glass and drink it in, I would. Only the girl is watching me, so instead I try to take everything in while walking towards the table very slowly. On his desk there is a pile of papers, a fountain pen, a clear paperweight that looks like someone has spilt coloured ink in a globe of water, and a photo of Busty Babs hugging the same beefy lad I recall from my encounter in the garden. To the left his computer flickers and to the right

I can see the remnants of his lunch. Dad ate sushi: actual uncooked fish with splats of yolk on top. When Dad lived with us he took me to the zoo and said raw fish was only suitable for penguins.

As I place the letters on his desk I hear a door open somewhere behind me. I swing around and grab a fleeting glimpse of Dad far across the room. For a second our eyes lock and liquid pain pours from mine, making a river over the desks between me and him. The current grows stronger, yet no one else seems to notice they're in the middle of it. For a second I half expect him to need a life jacket, because he's drowning in my hurt. Instead, he fires back out the door again and disappears into the maze. I'd like to run after him, but someone appears to have glued my feet to the floor without telling me. The girl who is with me disappears back out of the room, telling me to wait here. I stare at the pair of used chopsticks dotted with rice and I replace the lid on his fountain pen. The ink could leak onto his papers.

When the girl returns, she's a little less friendly than before. "I think you'd better finish up and go. You're done for today and, in fact, you're done for every day. Malcolm didn't have anyone doing work experience for him."

"He's m-m-my dad," I stammer.

"You've got some imagination." She folds her arms and I notice the stud in her nose is in the shape of a dragonfly. "Malcolm said he didn't know who you were. Now you're telling me he's your father. I'm not sure what your game is, but if you want proper work experience you need to write in. You can't just wander in off the street. Did you speak to the receptionist?" She's so annoyed I think her dragonfly is about to go bang, with all its legs shooting off in different directions.

"I'm related to Malcolm," I whisper. "Ask him

again. Perhaps he didn't recognize me at first. It's been a while."

"Look, I've met Malcolm's son. You're nothing like him."

I've lost the battle. Whatever I say she has an answer and I can't explain my whole family history while she's tapping her sheepskin boot on the tiles. Holding my hands up I say, "Okay, I'd better go now anyway because Mum is serving snails for dinner and I can't be late."

Snails? Man, why did I say that as she was dragging me from the office? It didn't even sound exotic, it just sounded gritty. The young woman escorts me down in the lift and out through reception. I'm half expecting all the silver bells to ring on the Christmas tree and proclaim me a stalker. The receptionist looks at me as I'm frogmarched past a bowl of purple orchids. I think a flower head falls as I waft past.

"Don't come back either," says the young woman, pushing me out into the street and closing the door. The glass shard, it seems, is shut.

I dream of the Dad tree again. It's still standing. However, the branches are bending and breaking so much that I fear it is going to split apart. Glittering jet-black leaves rise high into the air before forming black clouds over Saint Gabriel. Then they fall again, covering my feet as if the sky has slipped to earth. Slowly they build up until they're around my middle. Higher they rise, until they're up to my shoulders and it's all I can do to force my hands up through them. My fingers stretch upwards and I see a hand reach for mine. It grips me and won't let go. I swear it is pulling me out of this and I strain to see Dad's face but it never becomes clear. But I know he's there. His touch is warm and the feeling is familiar and safe.

I never want this dream to end.

CHAPTER 15

A cardboard box of Big Dave's belongings appears in the hallway. I can see a few car manuals, a football, some zombie novels and a silver frame with a photo of a young boy inside. "That's Kit," says Big Dave, appearing behind me. He takes the frame in his hand. "He's my boy."

"Uh, okay," I reply, surprised that Big Dave doesn't seem to be keeping his son as much of a secret as I imagined he would. "You've never mentioned him before."

"Really?" Big Dave thinks about it for a second. "I thought I had."

I stare at the little boy in the picture. At a guess I'd say he's about five and he's got two plasters criss-crossing his knee, like an X marks the spot. To his left I can see a wafer-thin slice of a floral skirt, a bare leg and a flip-flopped foot. "Is that bit his mum?" I look again. She has cherry-red toenails.

Big Dave pops the frame back into the box. "I can't remember," he replies.

How can he not remember? I attempt to give him The Look, but Mrs Parfitt is far better at it than me. When The Look fails, I want to say *Liar, liar, pants on fire*, but I can't do that either because it might be a bit insensitive (seeing as his pants nearly *were* on fire, thanks to us). To start with, Mum was in shock about the whole fire incident but then she just kept asking: "Why did you leave a burning candle unattended?" Big Dave just shrugged. After the shock came the anger: Mum wanted to know why Big Dave was outside looking at his car tyres at the time. "Isn't that something you'd check when you're at the garage?" Mum gnawed away at it like a dog with a *Tyrannosaurus rex* bone. Big Dave glanced over at me and I knew that he knew I'd been up to something and it all felt a bit weird. But Big Dave didn't spill the beans about me being there on the night of the fire, even when Mum was revving up for the nag of her life.

"Football?" he says now.

"What?"

"You and me playing floodlit football." Big Dave picks up the ball from the box. "Your mum says there's thirty minutes before dinner's ready. Come on, a pound for the winner."

The street has been scattered with frosty stardust and our hot breath makes white air balloons rise in the chill air. We pull off our scarves and use them to mark out the goalposts. Street lamps throw hoops of gold onto our pitch and every time I run down the road and score a goal, Samson, who is prowling in Mrs Nunkoo's front garden, yaps. For half an hour I forget about Dad, Christopher, Jo, Grace and Mum. It's just me, Big Dave and the football.

"Gooooaaaalllll!" Big Dave screams, lifting up his coat over his head and running down the road whooping. He slips on some ice and I laugh so much that I have to bend over to stop my stomach spilling out of my trousers. "Oi, Dan, you're looking at the master." Big Dave straightens up and kneads his back before hobbling towards me. "Where do I sign to join the team for the World Cup?" This makes me laugh even harder – perhaps a tiny bit of wee escapes. It's hard to say.

"Do you play football with Kit?" I ask, grinning.

"Sometimes," mumbles Big Dave, smoothing his coat down. "But he's got a lot going on at the moment and I don't like to hurry him into doing things he doesn't want to."

"Hurry him into football?" My smile disappears.

"Sometimes you can't make someone do something they're not quite ready for. It's complicated…but when you're a parent you have to make the right decisions for your family. Do you understand?" Big Dave puffs out.

I don't but I nod anyway. Even if I have a lot going on, I'm always ready for football.

"You're going to meet him soon," says Dave. "I'm not sure if your mum has already mentioned it, but I'm sort of hoping to move in and you'd get to know Kit then."

For a moment I stand still in a halo of street light, trying to take in what Big Dave has just said. "You wouldn't mind me bringing Kit into your home, would you? I mean, if you hated the idea we'd try and organize something else. It's the rented house, you see, I've got to make arrangements to move out." I nod as he continues talking. "Kit's a good lad and I think you two will be the best of friends."

"Big Dave," I whisper, "everything is changing."

"Yes, I suppose it is, but changes aren't necessarily a bad thing." Big Dave throws an arm around my shoulder and pulls me into his body.

"I don't like change."

"I understand, but life can't stand still even if we wanted it to," replies Big Dave. "And those changes that seem so scary could lead to exciting things happening in your future."

"Like you and Kit moving in?"

Big Dave laughs and says, "Yes, like us moving in." He squeezes me so close that I can smell engine oil, damp wool and pine forests. "If these changes seem scary, promise you'll come and talk to me. I'll be there for you."

I promise but then an image of Dad pops into my mind and I feel guilty and pull away. Big Dave laughs then ruffles my hair.

"You're too old for a hug, eh?"

But I'm not. I want Dad to hug me more than anything in the world. If he appeared at the end of the road right now, I'd run towards him and open my arms wide. I'd fling myself into his body and I'd hold him and never let go.

"Come on, it's getting cold," says Big Dave, giving me back my scarf. "Let's go home."

"Thank you," I say.

"For the scarf?"

"Not that," I reply. "For not telling Mum it was me who asked you to check your car tyres."

"Oh." Big Dave sighs. "I have no idea what you're talking about. I've got a terrible memory." He winks and swings open the gate to 10 Paradise Parade.

Grace isn't so forgiving though. When she gets me alone upstairs after dinner, she asks me why I'm sucking up to Big Dave. "You know he's got a wife and child," she spits. To reinforce her point she pulls me into her bedroom and puts on the pink silk dressing gown. "Have you forgotten this?"

"No," I mutter. "But I'm allowed to play football."

"Sure." Grace bites her lip. "Make the most of it, because when Mum finds out what he's been up to she's going to bin him for definite. So play your football because, before long, he'll be out on his ear and the football will be going after him."

"Do you know what?" I say, anger crackling in my chest. "You can be pretty mean, even in your state."

"What state is that?" Grace twirls around in the dressing gown.

"Nothing, forget it," I reply as the dressing gown cord whips me in the stomach. "Pretend I never spoke."

"I already have," she mutters, smoothing down the silk.

"Big Dave told me about his son, Kit. I don't think it's a secret that he's got a child any more. There's talk of them moving into our house because his house got burned." I fold my arms.

Grace blows a raspberry. "That's what I think of that. I bet he didn't mention *Caroline 1973*, did he?" I shrug and Grace goes, "So, are you saying he didn't talk about his wife and they're still moving in with us? What kind of a two-timing monster is he?" Grace moves on to chewing the corner of her lip. "I mean there's no way you could have got things mixed up, is there?"

"Me?" My voice is so high I reckon all the dogs in the neighbourhood have just pricked up their ears. "What about you?"

"Well," says Grace defiantly, "my female intuition tells me he's still a sneaky cheater. A woman is never wrong. You'll learn that when you get older." She laughs as though she's given me some pearls of wisdom and then says, "You're welcome."

"You'd better take that dressing gown off before Mum catches you in it," I reply. "Wonder how easy it'll be to explain that you were in Big Dave's house just before it caught on fire. I mean, if you hadn't knocked over the candle in the first place, then Big

Dave wouldn't have to move in with us." I stare at her before adding, "You're welcome."

For once Grace actually looks as if she's been slapped in the face. It appears I have out-ninjaed the ninja. Slowly, she unpeels the dressing gown, folds it up and stuffs it back into her wardrobe. "Okay, you've made your point. It wasn't my fault that a candle got knocked over. Caroline shouldn't have been with Big Dave and then none of this would have happened. Anyway, forget about the fire. No one died and we've still got to tell Mum the truth."

"Not just yet," I plead. "Come downstairs in a minute and let's think about what to do next. I'll even pour you a juice." Grace's eyes narrow but when I flash a big gummy smile she nods. In the face of Dan Hope's intelligence, his enemies crumble. Well almost, because Grace says if I spit in her juice she will come into my bedroom when I'm sleeping and shave off my eyebrows.

"I can honestly say I will not spit in it," I reply.

I'm surprised that I forgot to do this and I'm also surprised at how easy it is to slip the crushed-up folic acid tablets into her glass. Grace isn't going to know a thing and from this point on she's going to be happy and healthy. "Here you go," I say when Grace comes into the kitchen. "A lovely freshly squeezed orange juice." I pass her the glass of juice and she takes a sip.

"What are you two up to?" asks Mum, wandering into the kitchen.

"Nothing," I reply, giving Mum my saintliest pose, as remembered from the poster of Saint Aloysius Gonzaga on Jo's wall. Admittedly, it's not easy to look towards heaven when you're trying to keep one eye on your sister.

Grace drinks from her glass and pulls a face. She takes another glug as I pretend not to notice her coughing and chewing. When it becomes impossible to ignore, Mum says, "What's wrong with you?"

"It's this orange juice, Mum. It's all gritty, I swear."

Mum reaches into the fridge and pulls out the carton of juice and reads the sell-by date. "It's not off. Anyway, it's orange juice with bits. That's what it says here. *Bits.*" Mum taps the carton with her fingertip before shoving it back in the fridge.

"Not added bits that taste like the bottom of a budgie's cage." Grace plonks the glass down on the table.

Before I can stop her, Mum does something silly. Marching over to the table, she picks up the glass of juice and then downs it in one. "Doesn't taste too bad," she says, looking unconvinced. Mum coughs a few times. "Perhaps it's a little gritty."

I appear to have poisoned my mother.

poison

> *n* **1** a substance that causes illness or death
> **2** something that has a destructive influence
> *v* **1** give poison to a person or animal
> **2** contaminate with poison **3** have a detrimental
> effect on another person: *to poison a person's mind*

Last night I spent hours listening to Mum snoring, just to make sure she hadn't died. I even got up at one in the morning, tiptoed downstairs, found the dictionary and brought it back to my bedroom to read the definition of poison. I think I fell asleep just after that, because I woke up in a dried puddle of drool with the word *poison* printed on my cheek. I tried to wash it off but some of it had set like concrete.

"You're alive," I say as Mum walks into the kitchen and pours herself a cup of tea.

"Just," replies Mum. "You haven't got rid of me yet."

I choke on my cereal and Grace thumps me on the back, saying, "I've just saved you from death by puffed rice. Don't feel you have to thank me. But if you want to, I've seen a new pair of pink tweezers you could buy me as a gift."

"Bushy eyebrows are in," I wheeze. "Don't you read anything in those magazines?"

"I would if I could get them off my little brother."

Just as I open my mouth to answer back Mum says, "Well, this chatter about eyebrows is just riveting and I'd love to stay and join in, but I've got a hospital appointment in an hour." Mum drains the last bit of tea and sets the cup down.

What? Did Mum just say she's got to go to the hospital this morning? Not only has she been feeling ill for ages but yesterday I just about finished her off by poisoning her with two folic acid tablets. This can't be good.

"After my appointment I'm going to put up all the Christmas decorations, and when you get home from school I'd like to have a lovely chat." Mum's eyes glitter with tears. It must be a symptom of poisoning. "Don't press me for information on what we'll be talking about though. My lips are zipped." Mum then snorts with laughter, which I take to mean the tablets have turned her hysterical. "Right, I've got to get off now or I'll be late for my appointment, but be good and if you can't be good, be amazing. Oh, and Dan, I'm not sure you can be totally amazing if you've got a tiny print of the word POO on your cheek."

As Mum leaves the house I wipe my cheek with my sleeve and ask Ninja Grace what she thinks is wrong. "You don't think she's been poisoned, do you?"

Grace has a bit of cereal stuck to her chin. It makes her look like a witch and I don't tell her it's there (which is the most fun I'm going to get for the day). Grace's eyes narrow. "Give me strength. Get rid of those detective stories you're always reading and get with the real world. It's probably women's troubles."

I don't ask what those troubles are because I've got enough men's troubles of my own. The most pressing one being: poisoning a woman with troubles.

I have to make sure Mum's okay. Grabbing my school bag, I leap up from the kitchen table, telling Grace it's already eight thirty-five so I'm off to school. I swear she's still shouting that I never go to school on time when I slam the front door behind me.

Up ahead, I see that Mum's only just made it to the end of Paradise Parade. I dive behind a privet hedge as she turns the corner. Thankfully, she doesn't spot me. And she still doesn't see me flinging my body behind wheelie bins and fences as she takes the alleyway towards the Ireland estate. I'm going in. I'm slipping through the shadows of the alleyway like Mum's much thinner shadow. Occasionally, Mum looks behind her, but I'm too quick to be spotted.

The Princess Rose Hospital is a huge university hospital three miles further east. It is in no way close to the houses on the Ireland estate. In fact, you can't even catch the 237 hospital bus from here. Mum hoists her bag further up her shoulder before heading down Carnation Road in the general direction of Big Dave's house. So far, she hasn't clocked me. She turns into Big Dave's street. As I'm hunkered down in a garden, I hear a doorbell parp further down the road. I bob up and then down again.

There's going to be a massive showdown. Mum has pitched up at Big Dave's house, as I suspected. Any minute now, *Caroline 1973* is going to answer the parping doorbell and find my mum standing there with her fancy sequined handbag and give her what for. All that's going be left of Mum will be sequins on the front lawn. My nose rests on the edge of a hedge as the front door flies open. One eye squeezes shut in a wince. Big Dave steps out into the daylight and snogs Mum full-frontal. Curtains all the way down the road twitch like a Mexican wave. Then they jump into his car and zoom away like two lovebirds in a...um...Mondeo.

Like Grace has said many times before, Big Dave is up to something, but I can't work it out. Where was Caroline? Didn't she mind Mum kissing her husband on the doorstep? The whole thing makes my head rotate and that's no good when you've got maths first thing.

Mrs Parfitt isn't impressed when I hand in my unfinished lines and then she asks why I didn't stay in the library to complete them. Mrs Parfitt, it seems, has spies everywhere. So I have to lie and say the inferno in Kevin's guts spread like wildfire and ended up in mine and I spent the rest of the afternoon on the toilet. Mrs Parfitt says the next time something like that happens can I please let a teacher know where I am. But I tell her that when you could poo through the eye of a needle you don't have time to let anyone know.

Kevin looks at me as if to say, *What the actual flip are you on about?* But we both know he can't argue because he used exactly the same story on Mrs Parfitt and if he says I'm lying then he must have been lying too.

Mrs Parfitt stays annoyed with me the whole morning. She says that as soon as she opens her mouth in the maths lesson, I switch off. And she says I'll get more lines if I don't start listening, pronto. She doesn't actually say pronto but that's what she means. But how can I take in mathematical problems when I'm trying to solve a problem of my own?

"Daniel, I won't tell you again."

The pressure builds up inside me as if I'm a dropped bottle of fizzy pop.

"Please pay attention."

I might explode with all these worries in my head. And if I'm fizzy pop, am I cola or lemonade?

"Daniel Hope. Are you listening?"

"Yes, of cola," I say. "I mean, of course." I feel my cheeks burn before I look over at Jo. Without smiling, she turns away. Ever since I tried to give the medal back and told her I didn't need her, she's been avoiding me.

"That was funny," whispers Christopher. I could swear he's happy that Jo is ignoring me.

"Right class – including you, Daniel – listen up. I have some phenomenal news that I've been saving for the right moment." Mrs Parfitt perches on the edge of her desk, her long skirt spilling down to the floor. "I told you you'd want to work hard on Project Eco Everywhere. There was a reason for that, and now I can reveal it: Project Eco Everywhere is going to be on TV."

The school roof is nearly taken off by a big whoop from the whole class.

"The local TV station have heard about Project Eco Everywhere and think it's a great idea, particularly at Christmas time when we waste so much. They want to come to the Amandine Hotel and film it. I imagine it will only be a small slot at the end of the news, but nonetheless this is fantastic. We might even see their new presenter at the show. Now, what's his name again?" Mrs Parfitt shuffles through a deck of papers.

And then she says it: Malcolm Maynard. There's a firework display inside my head.

My dad is coming to my show.

It's going to be the best moment ever. Things couldn't have worked out better if I'd planned them myself. When he saw me at the TV office it was a shock, which is why he ran off, but if I'm onstage he'll get the chance to see me properly.

Then rockets turn into damp squibs. I've just remembered I'm not going to be on the stage.

"Miss, Miss, Miss!" I raise my hand as high as it'll go.

"Yes, what can I do for you?"

"Please, Miss, do you think that I could go onstage instead of being behind the scenes? If I promise to be good, Miss. Please, Miss."

Mrs Parfitt says, "No, Dan, I do not think you can go onstage. I gave both you and Christopher a punishment and that still stands. Nothing has changed just because the TV cameras will be there."

Everything has changed, I tell myself. I try to hypnotize Mrs Parfitt because I remember Jo saying God helps those who help themselves. For ages I stare into Mrs Parfitt's eyes, trying to communicate my desperation. Her eyes are the colour of a stag beetle's back and she blinks rapidly, as if blocking my mega mindwaves. When I start pulling strained faces and staring even harder, she asks me if the gut inferno is still raging and do I need the toilet. I shake my head and look away, swallowed up by embarrassment and anger that God was no help whatsoever.

Someone behind me clears their throat. "Excuse me, Miss. What if we weren't fighting? What if you..." Christopher clears his throat again, "...were mistaken? What if we were play-fighting and it was a game?"

Mrs Parfitt looks baffled and then says, "Are you telling me I didn't look out the school window and see you fighting? Are you actually being truthful?"

Christopher flares red and it travels right up to the tips of his ears. "It was fun, not fighting."

"Don't be preposterous. I saw it with my own eyes and it was anything but fun." Mrs Parfitt adjusts her glasses. "That is my final word on it."

I repeat, "Please."

"No," Mrs Parfitt replies firmly.

"So no is your final word on it?" I ask.

"Yes."

"So yes is your final word on it?"

Apparently, "If you don't be quiet, you'll be going to the head's office" is her actual final word on it.

We are told to bring out our Project Eco Everywhere costumes and continue working on them. Even though I'm not going on the stage, I've made a pair of glasses from the cut-off bottoms of two plastic water bottles. When I put them on, not only do I look like a bluebottle, but I can see nine classrooms. Dad would be impressed. Nine Jos approach me with red half-blown-up balloons in one hand and scrunched-up tissues and pictures of a fire ripped from a celebrity magazine in the other.

"What's that?" I take off the plastic glasses and try to make conversation as Jo passes my desk.

"It's the sacred heart of Mary. I'm going to make tissue roses and wrap them round the balloon. Not that it's any of your business."

"What's with the fire picture from a magazine?" I ask. "I'm not sure the Virgin Mary would be interested in gossip."

"No," says Jo. "But her heart was burning so this is the closest I could get. And can you please stop talking to me as I'm very busy." She puts a tea towel on her head before walking away.

Meanwhile, Kevin has a pair of holey underpants on over his trousers and is cutting up an old furry blanket, while Mrs Parfitt moves in to stop him, horrified that he's using his lap as a cutting table. Saleem is struggling with loads of toilet roll (unused). And Christopher is drawing on his arm. I take a bit of wrapping foil and make a star and then squeeze it between my fingers until it crumples and I feel better.

At lunchtime Jo blanks me but Christopher waves me over to the gravel football pitch. "Come and play footie with us. We're a man down. You can go in goal."

I throw my scarf and gloves into a small heap and run towards Christopher. "Thanks," I say.

"On me head, Saleem," he shouts, bobbing up. "On me head." Saleem kicks the ball and it travels towards Christopher, before he heads it away again. "Kick it in their goal. Awww, c'mon, are you blind?"

"Thank you," I echo. "For telling Mrs Parfitt we were just playing."

"Ref! That was handball." Then to me: "We were, weren't we?" Christopher skirts around the edge of the goal and I wave my arms about as though I'm swatting a cloud of flies. "Anyway, why are you so desperate to be in the Project Eco Everywhere show?" Christopher stops.

"I just wanted to be on TV, that's all," I say indignantly. When the football comes bombing in my direction it takes me by surprise. I forget to swat the flies and don't manage to catch the ball with my hands, although I do save it with my stomach.

"Well saved," says Christopher, helping me up. "It didn't work anyway. We've still got to stay behind the scenes and it's going to be boring."

"Perhaps it doesn't have to be," I say, grinning through the agony. "I have the brightest idea ever."

CHAPTER 17

When we get home that afternoon, tinsel drapes from the ceiling and flutters down the walls, and the soft thump of a Christmas CD fills the living room. And in the corner, near the front window, a lopsided fir tree has appeared, with lots of coloured boxes underneath. I've definitely given up on getting a new bike, which is just as well, because the small present with my name on it is only the size of my palm. Riding a bike that tiny would qualify me to join a flea circus. A comforting waft of warm, spicy gingerbread comes from the kitchen – Mum has lit the fire and flames crackle and lick up the chimney.

"I'm glad you're both home," says Mum, entering the room and wiping her hands on a tea towel. "I've got news."

So you've pictured the perfect scene of family life. Now toss it from your mind, because when Mum offers us a gingerbread biscuit she's baked we nearly choke on the overload of spices, and then a bit of tinsel falls off the mantelpiece and dangles into the fire and starts melting. Mum pulls it out again and begins whacking it with the tea towel. Small bits of charred tinsel and cotton float up into the air.

"I wanted it to be special," says Mum, flopping back onto the sofa.

"It is special," I say, battering a stray frond of fiery tinsel with Grace's rolled-up magazine. "Stand down, everyone. The emergency is over!"

"Earlier today I told you I had a hospital appointment." Mum nibbles at another piece of gingerbread, only to fan her mouth and set the biscuit down again.

Grace looks at me and I look at her.

"All right, I can see I've kept you both waiting long enough. This is my news." Mum reaches into her handbag and brings out a photograph. "As you can see," she says, handing us the picture, "I'm having a..."

"Prawn?" I stare at the curled-up shrimp.

Turns out Mum is having a baby, not a prawn, although if you squint they could be one and the same thing. Apparently, its proper name is Little Dave. Seems Little Dave was a complete surprise, but a lovely one. Mum didn't realize she was pregnant and that was why she'd felt sick for so long. She says things are going to have to change around this house – we're going to have to tighten our belts a little bit (not that there is any chance of Mum tightening hers, judging by how much her stomach is expanding).

"So you're both having babies. Awkward," I say, before engaging my brain. Mum's mouth flies open and a missile of gingerbread lands on Grace's cheek. Then Grace jumps up from her seat and starts screeching. Turns out her horror is nothing to do with the gingerbread face mask and more to do with her thinking I'm an idiot. Spittle forms on her lips and her eyebrows thread together. The dog, sensing there is some sort of excitement in the living room, comes in, finds and eats some tinsel and then pukes on the carpet.

"Stop that," I shout as Charles Scallybones sniffs the sick and starts lapping it up. "You'll get tinselitis."

This is my best joke ever but no one laughs.

"I am not pregnant. Take that back." Grace leans into my face and I shrink away. "What do you think this is: the immaculate conception?"

"I found your pregnancy test in the bin." I glare at her and she glares at me. It's a Hope vs Hope face-off!

Well, this is enough to send her into orbit on a supersonic rocket. One minute she's glaring at me, the next she is bouncing off the walls, tearing at her ponytail and screaming that she doesn't deserve this. Within three seconds she has reached the moon and orbited it a few times before landing back on the sofa and repeatedly banging her head with the cushions. On the last bash Mum clears her throat, possibly of ginger but who knows.

"If you're quite finished, Grace," Mum says, "I think you can step away from the cushions. You could get ten years in jail for the death of soft furnishings." She smiles, turns to me and her cheeks colour pink. "The pregnancy test was obviously mine."

At this point the penny drops, from the height of a skyscraper. Of course it belonged to Mum. How could I have been so stupid? Charles Scallybones saves the day by diverting attention away from me with a bad case of retching and yawning. Mum has to hurry him into the hallway with the aid of her big toe on his bum.

When she returns she says, "Dan, I thought you knew it was my test because you sent me a text." Mum shrugs. "I thought you texting me was your way of telling me you'd discovered the truth. I didn't press you on it because I thought you needed time to get your head around it. I was certain you'd talk to me when you were ready."

"I didn't send the text..." I reply. "It was Charles Scallybones."

The dog wanders back into the living room with a tinsel moustache and sick trailing from his velvety muzzle. He looks at us as if to say: *Wha?*

"Oh great!" wails Grace. "Blame it on the dog. This whole house is crazy. I am an island of normality in an ocean of insanity." When Grace's face goes red as a baboon's bottom, I think that's the exact moment when everything becomes clear. She says, "Ohmigod! Stan broke up with me because *you* told him I was having a baby. All his stupid comments about me being tied up in nine months make sense now. I thought he'd lost the plot. But no, it was all because my brother is stupid and told him I was pregnant!"

"I didn't tell him," I stammer. "It was Kevin Cummings."

Grace is back in orbit. "Ohmiactualgod! You told Kevin Cummings!"

"Okay, okay." Mum holds her hands up. "Enough. We've all made mistakes and we're big enough to get over them. Daniel, please tell Grace you're sorry."

When I tell her I'm sorry Grace says hell would need to freeze over before my apology is accepted. Well, I think the devil must be sliding down the frozen hills of hell on a plastic bag at this moment, because when Mum mentions "losing pocket money" suddenly the apology is good enough. The thought of not being able to afford a new lash-lengthening mascara is clearly too much for Grace. From this point on though, I need to keep my eye on her, because Grace is giving me a look that tells me she's about to assassinate someone. Someone being me.

When Charles Scallybones licks Mum in the face and leaves some tinsel stuck to her lip gloss, it's the last straw. "Out," she squeals, dragging him into the kitchen with a warning to us not to kill each other before she gets back.

"As if I'd waste my time and energy on you," snaps Grace, pulling at the fringing on the cushions.

"It was a mistake," I say.

"You're a mistake. Mum having Big Dave's baby is a mistake. It's all a mistake," Grace says. "Now I don't know whether to show Mum the dressing gown or not. I've been waiting for the right moment but Mum being pregnant makes it more complicated." Grace gets up from the sofa and pats her stomach and says, "By the way, on which planet can a girl as thin as me be pregnant?"

Thankfully, before I can answer, I'm interrupted by Charles Scallybones barfing up something in the kitchen and Mum shouting, "Jesus, Mary and Joseph, this dog's stomach is no stronger than tracing paper."

"Looks like a job for you." Grace folds her arms, satisfied.

Dog sick is a funny thing. Considering dogs are only meant to eat dog food, you'd expect it to be brown and lumpy in the way a human always brings up carrots. But Charles Scallybones's sick is full of hidden treasure. Once I found one of my superhero toys, a bit of Grace's thong and a rubber gherkin from his hamburger toy in there. But the best time of all was when he'd eaten sweet wrappers and I thought he was sicking up actual gold nuggets. Today, though, it's just yellow foam, a few strands of silver tinsel and a tiny plastic reindeer that Mum uses to decorate the Christmas cake.

"I think you'd better take the dog out for a walk before he does any more damage to the carpet," says Mum. I nod as I give her back the reindeer.

★ ★ ★

While taking Charles Scallybones for his nightly pee-a-thon I come up with my best thoughts yet. Firstly, I'm going to be a big brother, therefore I will do the job well. (What I won't do is change nappies or handle diarrhoea of any description, although the only description is probably brown and runny.)

The second thought I have is about Christopher. Of course, it could be a bit early to say this, but I think we're back to being friends. The downside is I've lost Jo along the way. I'm not proud of the way I spoke to her, but I was confused. I need to think of a way we can start talking again. Tomorrow I'll make it up to her, because I miss Jo and her stories about her religious collection. (This in itself is a miracle because I didn't think it was possible to want to hear any more about her relics.)

My third thought is about Big Dave, and this is the most confusing of all. He's invited me to his car workshop and said he'll show me how to take apart an engine and put it back together. Even though I want to do this more than anything, Grace keeps giving me dirty looks. I don't need a crystal ball to know this is about the silky dressing-gown fiasco. Grace won't let Big Dave show us any kindness and if he does she attacks him with words. Occasionally, Big Dave looks like a melted rubber duck, but then he smiles as if Grace isn't the meanest person in the world. Which we all know she is.

Charles Scallybones suddenly changes course. Seems he's on a mission to go straight to the scout hut and pee there first. This time the door is closed but I can still hear a grunting contest going on inside. I lift Charles Scallybones up on top of an old discarded shopping trolley from Aladdin's and climb up after him. We peer in the window and see everyone in the tae kwon do class is bent over, touching their toes. So I blow on the glass and write 0˙1134 which is HELLO when you type it on an upside down calculator. The woman shouts out about perseverance and how it means having patience. When Christopher sees me, he sticks his hand up and I see him leave the hall.

"Oi, Dan." Christopher opens the door and peeps out. "I can't talk long because she thinks I'm in the toilet. We're getting ready for our grading."

"Grading sounds like doing tests at school, only you're in your pyjamas."

"Dobok!" says Christopher.

"Bless you." I laugh but Christopher doesn't because the woman is screaming from inside the hut that integrity is the quality of being honest and if you say you're going to the toilet then your bowels need to be getting a workout.

"Look, I've got to go now," says Christopher. "She's onto me. She's got eyes in the back of her head."

"And in the toilet bowl, by the sounds of it," I say.

"Yeah, you're not wrong. But I just wanted to let you know, I've been practising on the guitar like we agreed. You're right about sneaking them backstage. It's a great idea to make the time go quicker. In fact, it's even better than getting up onstage and pretending to be a hero. Who wants to do that anyway?"

"Not me," I reply, as the tae kwon do lady shouts Christopher's name. He scarpers and I blow some more steam on the window and write 1134 40 before climbing down from the trolley.

When I walk away, a cold mist settles inside my chest. My thoughts have turned to Dad again. I've grown up a lot since those first emails I sent. I've met his other son and not given him a knuckle sandwich for taking my dad. I've been to Dad's house and work. Slowly, I'm fitting into his life. Charles Scallybones stops to do pee number ten on Mrs Nunkoo's wall. As the moon, like a white marble, rolls out from behind a cloud, I have another thought.

Even though I've grown up a bit, I'm still the same old Dan Hope – but is he the same old Dad?

Jo looks surprised when I tell her to open her hand. "Don't even think about putting something horrible in there," she warns.

"Don't worry, it's nice." I drop the medal onto her palm. "Here, you've got Saint Gabriel of Our Lady of Sorrows back because I can tell you're sad."

Jo doesn't look all that impressed. "This is the second time you've tried to give me it back."

"Second time lucky," I reply.

"It's third time lucky. So you're all better now?" Jo gives me a stare that would crack a mirror.

I shuffle about a bit under her gaze. "I've got no worries about anything, if that's what you mean. Look at me: healed. Saint Gabriel of Our Lady of Sorrows did the trick. Thanks for lending it to me."

"This is definitely a miracle because it usually takes Saint Gabriel longer than this. In fact, most people have to go through total and utter sadness before they can see the light. That's what it says in my saint book. But if you're saying you're through all that, then brilliant."

"Um...yeah. I think that's what I'm saying."

"It's just that Saint Gabriel was a hero. Not in the

usual superhero way of winning battles against his enemies, but because of self-conquest. He was a hero because he conquered himself. So, I think if you truly believe in Saint Gabriel, he will heal you by helping you learn to heal yourself." On that note, Jo squeezes the medal in her hand and turns. "But if you're healed now..." The words hang in the air as she walks across the playground.

"Jo," I puff, running after her, "I'm sorry but I need the medal back. I gave it back too soon. And I'm sorry for not believing in you too."

Jo turns and hands it to me, then raps me on the head as if she's at the back of a wardrobe, checking for a magical kingdom. "I knew Dan Hope was still in there and I knew I could still reach him. Want to come over to mine one day soon? I could show you my entire collection of colour-coordinated rosary beads." Jo smiles at me, drawing her lips right back to her ears.

"Could Christopher come?" I spy him skulking about by the assembly hall and wave him over.

"Dan says you should join us after school one day. I'm showing off my religious collection, if you're interested?" says Jo.

Christopher nods and goes so red he is almost a candidate for spontaneous human combustion. That's when I leave them together to talk, because my name isn't Dan Gooseberry Hope. As I make my way to the wall at the far end of the playground, I stare at the medal of Saint Gabriel of Our Lady of Sorrows. "How are you going to help me find the answers when I don't even know what the questions are?"

Sunlight glints on Saint Gabriel and I swear he almost glows.

CHAPTER 18

Big Dave sets ricepaper, glue, birthday candles and a thin bamboo hoop in front of me. He goes all mysterious when I ask if it's his birthday. Why else would we need birthday candles? Carefully he cuts four shapes from the thin ricepaper and glues the edges, before joining them together.

"We've got to wait until it dries." Big Dave winks and wanders into the kitchen to make a cup of tea.

I sit at the table for ages, just staring. In fact, I think I actually watch the glue dry. As soon as it's dry I shout at Big Dave to come back and finish whatever it is he's making. All the while Big Dave works he doesn't say a word about what he's doing and why. Instead, I help when asked and watch when I'm not.

"It's a balloon," I yell as Big Dave attaches the bamboo hoop to the bottom of the ricepaper shell.

"No, it's better than that," replies Big Dave. "It's a sky lantern." I whoop when I realize we're going out to fly it. "Bring that dog of yours, because this is going to be fun," says Big Dave, handing me the lantern.

The sky is studded with stars and our breath rises into the night air. Big Dave leads the way, stalking through the estate and then through the scrubby land towards Skateboarding Hill. Beyond it I can see the wood and I know that Dad's house is further on, just through the trees. This time I don't feel the urge to go lurking in his garden. Instead I carry the paper lantern carefully in my hands as though it was a tiny kitten with soft pink pompom paws. There's no place in the world I'd rather be at this moment than flying a lantern into the December sky with Big Dave.

"My dad showed me how to make and fly these lanterns," says Big Dave, petting Charles Scallybones on the head. "And now I'm showing you. My dad was always doing stuff with me. We made lanterns, learned about the planets, took apart engines and that's where I got all my knowledge from. And I've tried to share that knowledge with Kit, but he's interested in other things."

"When he gets older he might be interested," I say.

"I doubt it," answers Big Dave, "but it doesn't matter, because whatever makes him happy makes me happy. I'm going to bring him over to your house so you can all get to know one another. At the moment it's difficult because Kit still needs time to adjust to all the changes in his life."

"So Kit finds change scary too?"

"Yes, he does and things haven't been easy this last year." Big Dave smiles before adding, "But we're a family and we get through it together."

There's an awkward silence when I wonder if "family" translates into "wife". And I want to ask him the truth but I can't seem to find the words. I stare into the huge expanse of sky, my thoughts whirling inside my mind like snow trapped in a shaken globe.

"Look," says Big Dave, pointing into the sky, "there's the Plough. Did you know it's sometimes called the Butcher's Cleaver or The Big Dipper?"

I shake my head.

"The skies are fascinating. That's why I bought you the planets mobile." Big Dave spins around with his arms outstretched until he's dizzy and lands on his back like an upside down beetle. Laughing, he says, "Spin until you fall. Try it."

Round and round I go until I can't stand any more and I stagger forwards and back and then land on the ground with the lantern in my hands. I'm breathless with laughter when I look up into the heavens. The sky is so enormous, so endless, that I feel tiny beneath it.

Big Dave starts moving his legs and arms. "Look!" he says. "I'm walking among the stars. I bet you didn't know you could do this. Quick, Dan, start moving or you'll fall off the earth and get sucked into the galaxy."

There's no question about it, Big Dave is wackadoodle. I pretend to walk while lying flat on my back. Every time I move my legs, Big Dave moves his faster. We start sky-running. My eyes focus on the brightest star, my legs cycling on an imaginary air bicycle. I work them harder until I feel the burn in my thighs. Big Dave's legs move faster still and he's punching his arms too. He says I'll have to work harder if I want to catch him up. No one wants to lose the race through the stars. In the end Big Dave looks like his body is having a jerky spasm.

"Oops, I've just stood on the Pole Star," shouts Big Dave.

I think for a moment. "Ouch! I've got a dead leg because I've tramped on the Butcher's Cleaver."

From deep inside Big Dave's throat I hear a laugh building and his legs flop down. "You won," he says. "Look over there." Big Dave suddenly points into the sky. "A shooting star. Make a wish."

Far above me a star skitters across the sky, leaving behind a hailstorm of silver sparkles.

I wish with all my heart that I had a dad who would pretend to run through the stars with me.

"Come on, if you've made your wish we need to fly this baby." Big Dave rises up and marches to a clearing that he says is perfect. "We have to avoid power lines, buildings and trees or anything else that could catch fire. You can't be too careful, you know." He hands me a pair of gloves and tells me to put them on to protect my hands.

Big Dave very carefully attaches the candles and lights them before handing the lantern to me with a warning not to let go until I feel the lantern tug in my hands. "Some people like to write messages on the ricepaper," he says. "Then they let their messages go. I suppose it's a nice thing to do if you've got something you want to get off your chest." The lantern is pulling away from me now and my fingers release their grip.

Up it flies, floating and dancing into the darkness like a golden dandelion clock on a breeze. Big Dave and I watch as it sways this way and that, before travelling higher and further. We follow it on foot, like two wise men and one sickly dog following the Star of Bethlehem. Snow begins to fall, settling on our heads like juicy flakes of dandruff.

Beyond us the sky lantern runs out of steam under the weight of snow and as the candle goes out, it floats back down to the ground. Charles Scallybones finds it but by the time we get there he's eaten some of the ricepaper. "Don't worry," says Big Dave, picking it up and shaking off the snowflakes, "we can always make another one. We've got all the time in the world."

As we walk home, I feel windswept and happy and Big Dave tells so many jokes that my jaws ache. In fact, we're still laughing when we get to 10 Paradise Parade and we laugh some more as we enter the living room. But when I see Grace with a face like a smacked kipper, I stop. While Mum asks if we had a good time, Grace slips from the room. When she returns it's hard not to gawp, because she stands in the middle of the living room and then begins ballerina-twirling and spinning, pink fabric billowing into the air and parachuting back down again.

"Is that a new dressing gown?" Mum peers over the newspaper.

My stomach falls onto the carpet with a splatter and Big Dave applauds and shouts, "Bravo!" (although I suspect this is more for Grace's performance than my stomach). Mum is laughing, but baffled. I'm horrified and keep making these hand-cutting motions.

"Don't do this," I hiss helplessly as Grace does a curtsey. But at that moment I know nothing will stop the word ninja on her mission.

"No, Mum. I didn't buy this dressing gown. Big Dave did," says Grace, bobbing back up. "I'm sorry, but it's the truth. You've always brought us up to be truthful with one another."

"I've got no idea what you're talking about." Big Dave scratches his arm and then runs his fingers across his bald head, which is now simmering like a boiling egg. "I've never seen that dressing gown in my life."

"That's odd," Grace puts a finger to the crease at the side of her lips, "because it came from your house. Actually, it came from your bedroom."

That's done it. If we had a load of pigeons in the living room, Grace would have just put a hungry tiger among them.

"Mum, *we* didn't want to tell you this." I hate how

Grace has just used the word *we*. "Big Dave has been lying to you. He's got a wife, no matter what he's told you. He's still living with her. This is her dressing gown and this is the evidence *we* got for you." There *we* go again. It was Grace's idea to break into Big Dave's house and I was carried along. It wasn't *we*, it was *her*.

"Okay…" Mum rolls the word around her tongue. "I didn't know you'd been invited to Big Dave's house." She folds the newspaper and sets it on the coffee table.

Big Dave is bubbling: soft-boiled, I'd say. "Grace, you're wrong. You'll realize you're making a fool of yourself." He glares at her. Yup! We've just reached hard-boiled Big Dave.

Mum echoes, "When were you at Big Dave's house?"

No one could blame Big Dave for telling Mum the truth about what happened on the night of the fire, but he doesn't. I bet he's worked out that I distracted him while Grace was inside stealing the dressing gown and turning his bedroom into a barbecue. Instead, Big Dave's head sinks down into his shoulders. All the while he's repeating that this is stupid, that he shouldn't need to explain himself. Apparently, he hasn't seen his wife for ages. He doesn't even know exactly where she is these days.

Grace's performance is almost finished. Almost. Before taking a final bow she wafts the pink robe under Mum's nose. "Smell this, Mum."

"Poison," Mum says archly.

"Exactly." Grace's eyes narrow. "Poy-zon."

Big Dave blusters and says he doesn't keep poison in the house. He flaps his arms and tells us he's not with his wife, as Mum's eyes brim with tears. Mum tells him her children wouldn't make it up. If they say he has a wife still living with him, then he must have. Mum delivers the final blow by saying her children are not telling lies and she believes them and nothing he says will make a difference. She needs time and space away from him. *Ding-ding!* The fight is over and Big Dave is out.

I recall the moment Dad walked into the hallway, opened the front door and slammed it shut. I remember thinking he'd come back, before the slow realization that he never would spread over me. Big Dave has just done the same thing. The door made a *flam* sound then a tinkle, as the force made the knocker on the front flip up and down again. The colour skids from my face and my heart sails into an iceberg. Here I am, sinking in the fear that I might not see Big Dave again, and the fun we had with the sky lantern seems a million miles away.

"It had to be done," says Grace when I confront her in her bedroom.

"You've sent away the person Mum loves," I say flatly.

"That's a bit rich. Are you sure it's not because *you're* starting to love him? All those secret meetings you've been having."

"We were only flying a lantern. You could have come. It doesn't mean anything." I bite my lip, knowing that I'm betraying him. It did mean something, I tell myself. I enjoyed it. Grace says she feels sorry for me because I'm letting him into my life and I'm going to get hurt again. "I'm not," I say fiercely. "If Big Dave had to leave for good then I could live without him. It's not as if he's my real dad."

"Yeah, well, we managed to live without *him* too." Grace shrugs.

I'd like to say something clever, something important, something that will express how I really feel, but there just aren't any words. The stupid thing is I'm only living without Dad because I have to. It's not my choice and it's not as if I haven't tried to contact him many times. If Dad was back in my life, everything would be good once more and I wouldn't care about pink dressing gowns. All I can do now is hope that Project Eco Everywhere is going to wave a magic wand and deliver Dad back into my arms.

"Dan, you can close the door on your way out. I've got to text Stan now." Grace pulls out her mobile and stares at the screen.

"You're back with him then?"

Grace's fingers move across the keypad. "Uh, yeah, we're dating again, no thanks to you. Stan understands that I'm at a disadvantage by having such a ridiculous brother. He didn't even believe Kevin Cummings anyway."

"But he dumped you."

"*Au contraire, mon stupido frère*. There was no dumpage. We had an amicable separation and he thought about dating another girl but he didn't because he accepts that I'm his one and only. During our..."

"Amicable separation," I repeat.

"Yeah," says Grace, "during that time I lost about two kilos through stress. Now I can get into my skinny jeans and Stan thinks I look hotter than ever. I've still got it." As if to prove her point, Grace shakes her booty, touches it with a finger, makes a hissing sound and points me to the door.

When I flop on my own bed and pick up the guitar, I let my fingers sing a sad song. Ribbons of music flow from my fingertips up through my arms.

When they reach my heart they wrap themselves around it so tightly that I feel an ache. Next door, from Mum's room, I can hear soft sobs and then the whoosh of tissues being pulled from a box. I want to go in but I don't know what to say. If Big Dave is still in love with *Caroline 1973* then I suppose it's better to feel the hurt now rather than later. Mum sobs again. I set down the guitar and rise from my bed and pad across to my door. My fingers touch the handle but I can't bring myself to turn it and go to comfort Mum. Instead, I walk to the window, wondering if there are any shooting stars I can wish on in the snowy sky.

Some of the little terrace houses on Paradise Parade are sugar-frosted with snow. Others glimmer with pinpricks of jewelled fairy light. Mrs Nunkoo's dog is covered in snowflakes and yapping at the full moon. I bet he secretly thinks he's a werewolf. I smile at such a daft thought but the smile soon drops when I see someone huddled in a pool of street light. Someone chunky and wearing what looks like a bad snow wig over their bald head, someone with their shoulders drooping and their head in their hands.

That someone looks a lot like Big Dave.

CHAPTER 19

Big Dave doesn't return the next day, or the day after. Mum says she asked him to stay away for a while. Said she needed to think about the future of her family, including the baby. Mum is sad. Yes, she hides it well but I know she's missing him. I want to tell her to contact Big Dave, because a baby needs a dad, but the words are prisoners inside my throat. Some days Mum forgets to make my packed lunch and I have to share Christopher's and Jo's sandwiches.

"Here, have some of my holy guacamole. Doesn't your mum make you food any more?" says Jo, passing me some bread with green sludge on it.

"She forgot to do it today," I reply, adding, "because she has a lot on her mind," for good measure.

"My dad gets like that sometimes. He can be grumpy too, although you'd think he'd be happy because he's got this new girlfriend," says Christopher.

"Is she nice?" asks Jo.

"I've never met her but I've spoken to her a few times on the phone, although not recently." Christopher bites into his sandwich, leaving a snail trail of peanut butter and jam on his chin. "Families are weird anyway."

"You should borrow my sister. She's as weird as they come."

"No, thanks," says Christopher. "I've got a hamster."

"Would you like to borrow my patron saint of lunch?" asks Jo, trying to lighten the mood. "It's Friar Tuck." She bursts out laughing and I dodge in case some holy guacamole makes a break for freedom.

"Things are going to get better," I say, more to myself than anyone else. "There's the Project Eco Everywhere show coming up and that's going to be the best moment of my life."

"Are you serious?" Jo splutters. "I didn't know you were into this modelling stuff. You never told me. Plus you're not even going to be onstage, are you?"

I realize I was thinking aloud. I'm not interested in modelling. I'm interested in meeting Dad. Christopher is busy wiping his chin and moaning about his dad working late and how his Aunty Yvonne has been staying with them for ever, Jo is preoccupied talking about how she thinks she is going to be discovered at Project Eco Everywhere and then whisked away to Paris to sign a modelling contract for a bazillionty pounds, and I'm preparing for an event of life-changing proportions. If only they knew how important this show really is.

Later in the afternoon, the class sets off for the Amandine Hotel. "We're going to get our bearings," says Mrs Parfitt, shooing us onto the school bus. "I want you to familiarize yourselves with the hotel. I will point out where you're going to be and at what stage of the proceedings you'll be expected to step onto the Project Eco Everywhere catwalk. At the end of the show, I'll allow everyone to go onstage for a bow. That includes Christopher and Daniel."

I almost jump up into the air and do a fist punch. I am going to see Dad after all. I'm not going to be behind the scenes the entire time. I'm going to get my moment in the spotlight, flooded by gold and with Dad clapping wildly when he sees me.

"There you go," whispers Jo as we find our seats on the bus, "good things do happen when you believe in saints."

I want to say this has nothing to do with saints, but I imagine that would be like bopping a baby fawn on the head. This is so exciting my legs will hardly bear my weight. All the way to the Amandine Hotel I'm planning my first conversation with Dad in my head. Of course, I will say all the right things. Dad will be impressed by how well I'm doing at school. He'll say he's sorry. Whatever he says I will forgive him, because he is my dad.

"What?" Jo flicks her head towards me while I look at her blankly. "You just said 'Dad'."

"Did I?"

"Yeah, you did." Jo looks back out of the bus window. "Out of the blue. We weren't even talking about anything."

I don't know why I do, but I begin telling Jo about my dad. Not the bit about how he's famous now, but how he was when he was a proper dad and living at 10 Paradise Parade. How we lived happily together and how Dad used to tell me stories at bedtime. My favourite was the one about the rainbow. He used to tell me that no one ever dies because they go over the rainbow. Just behind that arc of colour were lots of beautiful souls living in a dream world.

"But you can run up to a rainbow," says Jo, her eyes wide.

"Yes, but when you reach it, it disappears and turns up in another place, so it's like you know there are people there but when you try to touch them they evaporate. It's sort of a story, but I imagined the people were red, orange, yellow, green, blue, indigo and violet-coloured zombies, and that made it even more exciting."

Jo is silent for a long time and then says, "You never usually talk about your dad."

"He left us years ago," I say. "Walked out and never came back."

"But you're still in contact, right?" asks Jo.

"Oh look," I say, pointing. "We're here."

Spotting the Amandine Hotel is a cop-out and allows me to change the subject, which has got too uncomfortable. This position I'm in with Dad is a funny one. Sometimes it's like I'm on a see-saw and I'm in the middle and everything is balanced on either side of me. When I choose to talk about Dad the balance tips and the see-saw starts to tilt and I slide down towards the edge, and then I have to struggle to get it back to an equal balance. But I want to talk about Dad because not talking about him makes the see-saw ride seem flat and never-ending, like a life where staying silent is almost more painful than talking.

"Right, class, line up and get off the bus carefully, please." Mrs Parfitt herds us into duckling lines and leads us off the bus and straight into the ballroom of the Amandine Hotel.

If rooms could smell of money, then this one would. It has red velvet wallpaper that, when you stroke it, feels like the fuzz on a peach. Beneath us there is a polished wooden floor and high above our heads is a huge chandelier, dripping with thousands of crystal raindrops that dance in the breeze of twenty-eight excitable children. Straight ahead are heavy curtains falling in deep crimson folds and tied back with long golden tassels that look like Rapunzel's hair. Mrs Parfitt points to the curtains and says we're going to appear from behind those and walk down the catwalk, stop, then look into the audience and "smize".

"That's smile with your eyes," hisses Jo to me, "it's a phrase from Tyra Banks, the supermodel."

I frize back (frown with my eyes).

Saleem looks bored and Kevin is pretending to moonwalk, only he's got really squeaky trainers on and it sounds like he's strangling a mouse. We're still not talking since the whole episode of him telling Stan that Grace was pregnant. When Mrs Parfitt tells him to put a sock in it I have to chew the inside of my cheek to stop myself from laughing in his face.

"This", says Mrs Parfitt, leading us backstage, "is the room where it all happens."

The room where it all happens looks like a room where nothing happens. Against the wall there are empty rails for clothing. The wallpaper is blistered and the place stinks of stale sweat, fruit cocktail and toilet cleaner. To my left there is a discarded spotty sock and a rose hairband. Even the rose has been crushed and one of the petals has stuck to the edge of Mrs Parfitt's leopard-print pump, making it look as though the leopard has a pink tongue.

"On the night I'd like the class to come fully dressed, but if you need to attach wrapping foil or pie cases or whatever then you can do that backstage with Daniel and Christopher to help. Over there will be a table with a mirror. By the way, is everyone's hero attending? Everyone except Jo's heroine, that is."

Everyone choruses, "Yes." But me, I shout the loudest, because I know my dad will be in the audience too. Jo gives me a funny look, but before she gets the chance to say anything Mrs Parfitt asks if there are any questions. That shuts Jo up. Still, she squints at me and mouths that she thought my dad had walked out.

I ignore her because I'm zorbing in an invisible bubble of happiness. Next time I'm at the Amandine Hotel, standing under the glittering chandelier, my dad will be here too. I, Dan Hope, am going to be revealed as the son of a famous star. I, Dan Hope, will be living the dream.

Dear Grace and Dan,
Just having a little lie-down and, before you worry, it's nothing more than baby-building tiredness. Growing this little one is exhausting. Your dinner is already in the microwave and all you have to do is set it to four minutes and hit the button. When it pings take the food out and eat it. Not too quickly, mind, or you'll take the roof off your mouth — the microwave can turn food into molten lava. By the way, it's Aladdin's Comforting Cottage Pie. If you need me, knock on the bedroom door and I'll get up. Don't forget to do your homework.
Love Mum x

Not only does my stomach somersault at the thought of cottage pie, because that's what I thought Mum was cooking the night Dad left, but if I was reading between the lines of the note Mum has written, it would say I miss Big Dave and I want him back. I'm halfway up the stairs to talk to her when I stop and sit down. My head rests against the daffodils on the wallpaper. Maybe I shouldn't try to have this conversation with her. Perhaps I'll only make it worse if I tell her I saw him sitting outside our house. But I did see him and I think he might have been crying.

Later that evening I take Charles Scallybones on his nightly toilet trip. Past the eerily silent scout hut then over the slushy wasteground we march, up Skateboarding Hill and down again, beyond the spot where Big Dave and I flew the sky lantern. And it's the thought of the sky lantern that makes me decide to find Big Dave and tell him how much he means to Mum. If I plead with him he'll come back and explain the truth about Caroline, and Mum will get out of bed instead of leaving fiery gristle in the microwave.

Big Dave's house has a LET BY sign forced into the grass and his silver Mondeo is parked in the usual spot. The curtains are open and I can see cardboard boxes on the window ledge. Big Dave suddenly flashes into my vision and comes to the window and peers out into the street for a second. I duck down behind a wall, which is ridiculous when you think about it, because I've come to talk to him. Big Dave pulls the curtains shut.

I hang around for ten minutes, trying to pluck up the courage to ring the doorbell. At the moment I think I've built myself up enough, the front door flies open. A woman steps out into the cool night air and pauses as Big Dave lounges against the door frame. They have a conversation but I can't hear much more than the word "Kit". The woman has brown hair cut so bluntly I imagine she could saw her own shoulder blades in half. She's wearing a black and white stripy coat that reminds me of a zebra. As she raises her hand and runs it through her hair, she leans back towards Big Dave. They're going to kiss, it's a dead cert. Big Dave moves towards her and clasps her shoulders as I squeeze my eyes shut. When I open them, Big Dave and his wife have moved apart and she is walking down the pathway, blowing more kisses.

Oh Big Dave, you've blown it now.

CHAPTER 20

The day after that, Christopher and I spend our morning break firming up plans to bring our guitars to the Project Eco Everywhere show. We're not going to waste our time sitting between old pie cases, oh no. We agree on playing "Over the Rainbow" because that's the only tune I know off by heart. Christopher says he has played it a few times, but he'll bring along his music book just in case he's rusty.

Jo sees us whispering and wanders over to ask us what we're up to. Christopher looks shifty but tells her it's nothing. "Why are you keeping secrets?" she asks, throwing a gum wrapper into the bin.

"There isn't a secret," I say.

"You'll get struck down by lightning if you're lying and Saint Barbara won't help." Before I can ask who Saint Barbara is, Jo offers, "She's the patron saint against thunder and lightning, by the way."

Of course she is.

"We're talking about the Project Eco Everywhere show," Christopher finally admits. "We're just deciding what to do when we're backstage."

Out of her blazer, Jo pulls a plastic card with a prayer on it, a piece of Lourdes rock, a small statue of Saint Anthony, an unused tissue, a string of blood-red rosary beads and a tropical lip balm, which she rolls over her lips. "I'm more worried about being on the actual stage. I've got a whole beauty routine to start tonight: cleanse, tone and moisturize. I cannot get a spot."

"Can't you wash your face in holy water? Surely that'll stop you getting a spot," I say.

"One cannot use religious items for everything," she retorts. "Then when you need help they won't be there for you. I've told you before."

I'm sorry I even asked.

Jo wraps her hair around her finger and says, "I've got to look beautiful on the Project Eco Everywhere catwalk."

"You don't need to worry, Jo," replies Christopher, "because you're already..." Then he stops mid-sentence. "You're already good at walking." He looks like he's about to sprint away in embarrassment. "I mean, on the Project Eco Everywhere catwalk," he explains. "You'll be able to put one foot in front of the other."

Please, ground, open and swallow him up.

"Yeah, that makes sense." Jo gives him a quizzical look before walking off. "I suppose I've had eleven years' practice," she calls back.

I burst out laughing. "She's not particularly amazing at walking. Why did you say that?"

"Because I keep opening my mouth and saying the wrong thing," Christopher replies. "And that annoys me. Everything does at the moment."

I stare at him, my eyes wide. Obviously there's something bothering him, so I ask if there's a problem I can help with. At first he says there isn't and then he walks across the school playground and sits down on the frosty stone steps, near the water fountain. I join him. For a while, neither of us speaks. Christopher fiddles with his school tie, rolling it up and down, while I concentrate on various children trying to get the water fountain to work, even though it's icier than an ice pop in Iceland.

"Yes, okay, I have a problem," Christopher finally

offers, kicking some glistening leaves from the steps. "I suppose I might as well tell you. It's my dad. A while back he said we'd need to move again. And I don't want all this. It's happening too quickly." He shrugs.

I rest my hand on his arm for a second then take it away in case anyone sees me. "Sorry." I blurt the word out.

"Don't worry, I can put up with it. At least I wouldn't have to change schools if it happened. My Aunty Yvonne said it'd be a good change. But what does she know? She doesn't have to move into a stranger's house and be all happy about it. I refused to go when Dad mentioned it at first and he said he'd give me more time." Christopher makes a Swiss roll with his school tie. "He's in a really bad mood. I think it's because of me, opening my mouth and making everything difficult. Dad says his girlfriend is lovely and she isn't a stranger because I've spoken to her on the phone, but that's not the point. I'd like my mum back."

"Oh."

"She left me." Christopher lets his tie unfurl.

"Left you?"

"Packed her bags and moved to Scotland with the man from Human Resources where she used to work. She didn't take me with her. Apparently, it was better for me to stay where I was settled." Christopher's eyes glisten but he tilts his head back far enough for his tears to disappear back inside. "Six months ago, I saved up some money and tried to buy a ticket to Edinburgh, only the man at the train station wouldn't sell me one. Said I was too young to travel all that way on my own. I'd even packed a bottle of Irn-Bru and a packet of shortbread. They like that in Scotland, you know." Christopher gives me a small smile and wipes his nose with his index finger. "In the end I had to go back home and picnic on the front step before ripping up the note to Dad that said I was emigrating."

"Oh," I echo.

"That's why I took up tae kwon do, you know." Christopher runs his fingers through his hair. "I thought if I ever met the man from Human Resources I could..."

"Kill him with your little finger?"

"Yup, something like that."

Christopher rises up and wipes the damp from the seat of his trousers. "But that's not even what tae kwon do is about. So Catriona can stay in Scotland with her boyfriend and I'll just get on with my life."

"Who's Catriona?"

"That's my mum. I don't even like calling her 'mum' any more. She doesn't deserve it."

"You're right," I say, jumping up. My bum feels a bit clammy. "She's missing out. You're better off without her."

Only I don't believe those words, because having no mother must be terrible. That's why he made his dad his hero. Everything fits now. But no matter how awful his mother is, I can understand why he wants her back in his life. In fact, I understand his pain so completely that I feel an unexpected and uncontrollable pang in my stomach.

Today is show day. Everything is going to be perfect. Everything except the weather, that is, because right now there's a monsoon raging outside. Like an angry monster, it whips leaves, batters trees until their limbs snap and then blows out great gusts of water. Somewhere in the distance there is a low thunderous growl, and Mum pulls back the net curtain and stares out at aluminium skies. From her expression, she isn't impressed. For ten minutes she walks up and down, worrying about us going out in a storm.

"It'll be okay, Mum," I say, pulling on my coat. "It's only water. I can't miss the show because of the rain. Mrs Parfitt will go ape if I'm not there. She's relying on me to help backstage. Without me, the whole show will go down."

"I know you're important." Mum fluffs my hair before returning to the window. "But it's torrential out there and I can hear thunder in the distance. I was certain they'd cancel."

"They can't cancel." I blink back the fear. "There's no way they can do that."

"Why not?" asks Ninja Grace, whacking me on the head.

"They just can't, that's all."

"At this rate we could join Noah on the Ark." Mum sighs and reaches for her coat and bag. "Well, if you insist it's still happening then there's a bus at the end of the road in four minutes. We need to be on it or we'll have to row there."

I pick up my guitar and the plastic glasses and tell them to hurry up because we can't miss that bus. Tonight is going to be my night.

"The guitar, what's that for?" Grace plucks one of the strings and the guitar protests.

I touch my nose and smile.

We catch the 36 bus, which will take us from Paradise Parade directly to the Amandine Hotel. Mum calls it the QTW bus: Quicker To Walk. That's because it stops at every lamp post and tree on the route. As if to prove the point, a soggy boy-racer pensioner on a mobility scooter manages to overtake us, and by the time we've reached the end of the road we're eating his dust.

"Stan can't come," says Grace, checking her mobile phone. "He's watching the end of his favourite quiz show. Someone is going to win either 1p or £100,000."

"I wouldn't want to be responsible for him missing that," I say, staring out the window as rain turns the street into a kaleidoscope of grey.

When we eventually reach it, the Amandine Hotel is blurred by a veil of pelting water. Flinging my guitar over my shoulder, I hop off the bus, waving at Mum and Grace and shouting to them that I've got to go backstage and they should grab a seat in the ballroom. Grace screams back something about breaking a leg, which doesn't seem entirely impossible as I hurry through the rain arrows. I arrive at the small black door at the side of the building and let myself into the darkened corridor leading to the backstage room where we are to meet.

Before anyone spots me, I slide my guitar behind a velvet curtain and then present myself to Mrs Parfitt.

"You're soaking wet." Mrs Parfitt ticks my name off using a red pen.

"It's raining, Miss."

"I gathered that much."

"But the show must go on, Miss."

"Indeed." Mrs Parfitt looks up from her clipboard. "You're very keen, Daniel. I must say, I like this. Considering you're not on the stage, it is nice to see you embrace the job you've been given. You'll still get your moment, I'll make sure of it."

"Thank you, Miss." A dribble of rainwater runs down my forehead and along the length of my nose, where it hangs like a gymnast on the rings.

While I'm talking to Mrs Parfitt I spy Christopher sneak his guitar behind the same curtain where I put mine. He gives me the thumbs up and begins whistling "Over the Rainbow" as he merges with our other classmates.

Jo turns up a minute later looking like the Virgin Mary, if the Virgin Mary was wearing a soaking wet tea towel and had a chicken pie foil case attached to her head to look like a halo. Saleem is a mass of wet toilet roll and says he's his mummy if she got caught in a monsoon. Kevin arrives looking like a soggy yeti. He's wrapped in the brown furry blanket and the underpants over his trousers are so wet they're slapping his knees. When Mrs Parfitt asks him to repeat who his hero is and how this woolly mammoth look represents them, Kevin reminds her it is his dad. Even though Mrs Parfitt doesn't probe any further, Kevin volunteers the information that his dad has a hairy chest all the way down to his— Mrs Parfitt puts her hand in the air to stop him from going further.

"I was going to say toes," says Kevin.

As soon as I get the chance to escape, I lope over to the curtain separating us from the audience. My finger teases the fabric aside and I can see Mum in the second row. Already she has a tissue crumpled between her hands. Every so often she dabs at her eyes. The seat beside her is empty – Grace has gone off who knows where. Row after row of faces build behind Mum and, despite trying to scan them all in ten seconds, I can't see Dad. What I can see is a TV camera at the back of the hall and it's focusing on the chandelier, which is throwing silver smudges into the audience, making them look like they've got sequined chickenpox.

"Gimme a look." Christopher jumps on my back and the curtains shudder, nearly sending us both flying onto the stage.

"Get off." I nudge him away and look out again. At the back of the ballroom I see Big Dave slipping in and taking a seat in the last row. I'm surprised at how nice it feels to see him again. Mum didn't say he was coming to see me, but then again they don't seem to be on speaking terms at the moment.

"For the love of God," barks Mrs Parfitt, pulling me back. "What if someone sees you?"

"No one saw me, Mrs Parfitt, not even my mother, who was waving at me from row two."

"Go and help the others prepare their costumes. Now scoot." I take Mrs Parfitt's advice and scoot as far away from her as I can, which means scooting straight into a corner. That's when something strange happens. In the half-darkness, I scent spearmint chewing gum.

"It's me, backstage boy," whispers Ninja Grace. "I've only got a second because I said I was going to the loo. If I'm not back soon, Mum will send out a search party." I doubt this very much, because Grace never goes to the toilet for just a second. Not ever. But that's not the main thing concerning me. The main thing concerning me is that Grace wouldn't have come backstage unless she had something important to tell me. I think my perfect day is about to be destroyed by the ninja. What if Grace says Mum wants to go straight home because the weather is getting worse? Or what if Mrs Parfitt has decided to cancel and not told us yet? Worse still, what if a massive bolt of lightning has broken the TV cameras and the crew have suddenly decided to go home? Grace stares at me and pulls a strand of chewing gum from her mouth and winds it around her finger.

"Why are you here?" I ask.

"You are not going to believe who is out there!"
The chewing gum unravels.

CHAPTER 21

I'm so open-mouthed I could hold a giant spaghetti hoop between my lips. "You just stick with the slack-jawed idiot impersonation while I carry on talking," Grace says, putting a finger to my lips. She takes a breath. "Dad is in the audience."

There is this strange silence just before my bowels start doing funny things. Most days you don't notice bowels, but on the odd occasion, like now, they fizz away to remind you that they can easily destroy you. Grace grasps my shoulders and asks me if I heard what she said.

"Yeah," I say, letting my eyes grow wide like flying saucers.

"Yeah? Is that all you can say? Our dad is here in the audience. Right here, right now. It is mental. I'm not going to talk to him. I'm going to snub him if he looks at me. So far he hasn't clocked us, but when he does he's getting a dirty look direct from me." Ninja Grace starts going on about how he is thinner in the flesh and how TV puts ten pounds on you. I'm not listening, to be honest. I'm too busy thinking there's an astronaut in my stomach and he's bobbing about in zero gravity.

Dad is definitely here. It is confirmed. It is S-U-P-E-R-M-A-S-S-I-V-E in capital letters.

"Snap out of it," hisses Grace, looking around to see if anyone has noticed her. "I've got to go now but I'm warning you not to make a scene. Mum's pregnant, remember." She leaves me in a minty fog as she sneaks back out into the ballroom.

When she's gone, I edge back to the curtain and look out again. Grace is taking her seat and mouthing rude words at me and just as I'm mouthing something back, Old Elephant Knuckles drags me away from the curtain.

"If I've told you once, I've told you…" I'm thinking *twice*, when Mrs Parfitt says "a million times". Sadly, teachers aren't what they used to be, because they cannot tell the difference between two and one million. I think about reminding Mrs Parfitt about

222

hyperbole, but instead I bite my lip a million times (twice) and promise not to go near the curtain again. She tells me that she's within her rights to stop me taking a bow, but when she hears Kevin shout that his underpants are so wet that they're going to trip him up she rushes off, muttering about health and safety.

Less than fifteen minutes later the backstage area is completely deserted, except for Christopher and me and our two guitars. "I like the rain," I say, my fingers plucking the strings to make them sound like raindrops.

"Me too," says Christopher, playing his guitar. "You were right about bringing these." Music zaps from our fingers like an awesome superpower. Accompanying us, raindrops drum a rhythm against the window and the rumble of thunder acts as a huge crescendo. Angry flashes turn the room negative and another massive rip of thunder tears the night sky apart.

Then the world goes black.

Silence drapes over us until a small voice squeaks, "Dan, my eyes have gone funny. I can't see a thing. Help me!"

"It's a power cut," I say, blinking through black.

"What's that?"

"I dunno, but I think we wait until the lights come back on."

Only they don't. Not immediately anyway and we stand in blackness so dense that it's like midnight. To my left I hear a door open and a blade of torchlight swings up towards my face. "Boys, it's a power cut, that's all," says Mrs Parfitt. "Mind you, the audience weren't sure at first. They saw the Virgin Mary glide down the catwalk and then everything went black. Someone shouted it was the Second Coming and I had to shout back that it was a power cut. Anyway, the lights will come back but we're not sure when. Unfortunately, the audience are getting fidgety." I hear a long sigh and a sniff.

"Dan could make it better." The torchlight swings towards Christopher, then back to me.

"How?" I hear myself ask the question.

Christopher says his idea relies on none other than the talents of good Daniel Hope. This turn of events horrifies me. Christopher has gone mad. In his mind he's omitted an O from his statement. Clearly, he doesn't think I'm good, he thinks I'm GOD. What can I do about a thunderstorm?

Mrs Parfitt clears her throat. "And how, might I ask, is Daniel going to entertain a whole audience sitting in total darkness?" *Yes, Christopher, I think, how am I going to do that?*

Christopher begins to play "Over the Rainbow", stumbling over some of the notes. "This is what he's going to do. He's brilliant at playing this tune. Put him out onstage and let him play, Miss. The audience might have lost their sense of sight but they can still hear."

Before I know what's happening, I'm standing at the side of the stage and Mrs Parfitt is introducing me to a clapping audience.

There is a chair centre stage and Mrs Parfitt has passed the torch to Yeti Man Kevin, who is going to highlight me for the duration of the performance. I shuffle out onto the stage and take my seat in a thin circle of light. Once, a while back, Mrs Parfitt told us if we ever had to give a speech or a performance we should imagine communicating with one person only. In my mind this one is for Dad, who at this moment is sitting in the darkness, and I am in the light at last.

As my fingers find the strings, the circle of torchlight zooms up to the ceiling then skates back across the floor before it finds me again. There is an audible sigh of relief from the audience and then a wave of laughter as Kevin shouts, "Oops, my fault, butterfingers. I'm sweating like a gorilla in a sauna in this fur."

I find the first chord and begin to play "Over the Rainbow". And for a while it goes pretty well. And then my mind wanders off to the last time Dad was in Paradise Parade. A memory comes back to me and it is one I've tried to squash for four years. I saw Dad leave that night. I remember it clearly now. I was sitting at the top of the stairs as he stormed into the hallway. I called to him and he looked up at me, a small shivering figure in asteroid pyjamas. Dad came up the stairs and whispered "Goodbye" into my ear. I gripped his jacket but he pulled away until my fingers lost their hold. Then Dad walked back down the stairs, and even though I called him once more, he didn't turn around. He left, slamming the front door, and I rested my head among the frilly daffodils.

My finger hits a wrong chord and then another. Kevin shakes the light as if it will somehow wake me out of a trance. It does, but not in a good way. I hit more wrong notes and can't find my way back to the tune. My hands fly off the guitar and a snooker ball pots itself into the back of my throat. Despite wanting to say sorry, I can't. My throat won't let me.

Soft footsteps echo behind me and I know, without turning, that Mrs Parfitt has come to whisk me off the stage. If she had a giant hook, she'd probably flick it round my neck and whip me off so fast my feet wouldn't touch the ground. The footsteps grow louder. With a forced grin and tears in my eyes, I prepare to get up and slink away. A firm hand clasps my shoulder and forces me back into the seat. What is Mrs Parfitt doing? The music of "Over the Rainbow" wraps around me like a warm duvet and as I turn, Christopher gives me a sympathetic nod.

He leads me along the pathway of the tune as I begin to play the chords again. Together we are strong and the liquid music pours through the audience and I can feel them urging us on. Dad can't think I'm a failure now. Perhaps he'll think it was all part of the act: me pretending not to be able to play, then suddenly I'm amazing. It's no different to those reality shows where the person is nervous and everyone thinks they'll be rubbish but then they open their mouths and they're phenomenal and everyone gives them a standing ovation.

We get our standing ovation too. Row upon row of chairs scrape as the audience jump to their feet and shout for more. Rather than disappoint, we do it again. In fact, we play it twice more and the final time the audience begin to sing and we both feel confident enough to walk around the stage (much to Kevin's displeasure, because it's hard to get one torch on two people at different ends of the stage).

When it's over, Mrs Parfitt pads onto the Project Eco Everywhere catwalk and thanks us for our impromptu concert and the audience for not leaving after the Second Coming. She laughs and Kevin angles the torch so the light is under Mrs Parfitt's chin. The shadows make her look like a scary beast. Mrs Parfitt, suddenly aware that the audience are shrinking back in horror, frowns and signals Kevin to switch off the torch. Once again the stage is plunged into night and Christopher and I have to crawl off on our knees because we're afraid of tripping and falling off the catwalk.

At last, when the electricity comes back, we're backstage and the whole class is buzzing around us with excitement. "You were all kinds of awesome," says Jo. "It was like the real Virgin Mary was in the audience and saw everything go wrong and made a miracle happen."

"That's one way to look at it," I say, moving away from her because her head smells like roast chicken.

"Seriously," says Yeti Man Kevin. He wipes some sweat from his upper lip. "That was the best. Do you need an agent, or even a torch technician? For a small fee…" Before I can say anything, Mrs Parfitt approaches and the whole class parts like string cheese.

"Daniel, you are a credit to this school." She stops in front of me and grins. Further back, someone clears their throat and Mrs Parfitt flips around and says, "And, Christopher, I haven't forgotten how you helped a friend in need. I am proud of you too. Now I want everyone to take a bow. The lights are back on, so it's your moment."

This is it!

We walk, arms connected, onto the Project Eco Everywhere stage, as the audience holler and whistle. One by one we take a bow. I'm sure we're there for at least five minutes and all the while I'm staring at every single face in the audience. Mum is waving a wet hankie and shouting, "That's my boy. He's the guitar player." When someone behind tells her to shush, she yelps, "You can't shush me, I'm gestating." But where is Dad? I'm certain he's not there. (Neither is the Virgin Mary, but then I wasn't really expecting her.)

The second I'm off the stage I grab my coat and guitar and race into the ballroom to find Dad before he leaves the building. Malcolm Maynard, TV star – Dad – is going to be standing under the glittering chandelier, waiting for my autograph. We're going to meet at last.

This is like the movies.

CHAPTER 22

This is not like the movies. The ballroom is almost empty and a constellation of stars have fallen from the ceiling and been trampled underfoot. Around the room, programmes have been scattered as if they were dominoes and someone knocked down one and the rest fell over in a chain reaction. While Mum chats to Mrs Parfitt, I dash through the remaining stragglers looking for Dad, but he isn't there.

He's got to be in the toilet.

Grace appears from the Ladies as I run towards the Gents. "Hey," she says, blowing a bubble with her gum. "You're in a hurry. You were okay up on that stage. Mum was in floods. Mind you, she's pregnant and will cry at anything."

"Was Dad impressed?"

"Dad?" The bubble bursts on her lips.

"What did he think of me?" I whisper.

I watch her, wondering what she's going to say next. Instead of words, she takes my hand in hers.

"No," I mutter. "No. No. No."

"Dan, listen to me."

"No," I repeat. "No, please don't say it."

"I've told you before, Dad isn't worth it. He walked out right at the beginning when he read the names in the programme. He must have seen your name and I'm sorry but I have to say it like it is: Dad is no good for us." Grace's voice drops away to nothing.

"He didn't see me on the stage?" Grace shakes her head. "Didn't hear me play guitar?" Her dark ponytail swishes from side to side. "Doesn't he love me any more?" Grace doesn't move her head but her eyes look away. Looking away in body language terms means I'm right. Dad doesn't love me. The guitar slips from my fingers and makes a soft clunk as it falls onto the ivy-patterned carpet. There it lies, choked and silent. Tears prick my eyes as I run towards the front door of the Amandine Hotel.

The air is sharp like sour candy and I inhale, then cough. At this moment I realize I have to get as far away from the Amandine Hotel as possible. I sprint down the driveway while Grace shouts from the front door, telling me to come back because she can't run after me because her gladiator sandals are no good in the rain. "They were in the winter sale," she screams. "Half price."

I run like I've never run before. Houses blur, trees are woody smears, and bruised clouds are crying tears on me. As the rain drenches my face, it's impossible to tell which tears come from the clouds and which are my own.

Dad has destroyed my night, stamped on my moment, poured more weedkiller on the little tree growing inside my soul.

Rivers flood the gutters and I tear through them, my feet bursting their inky dams. And I tell myself if I don't stand on the cracks in the pavement Dad will come back. Zigzagging along, I scream in frustration when I hit a crack.

"He won't come back now because you've jinxed yourself!" I yell. "It's your fault." I run faster. "It isn't my fault. It isn't. It isn't. He'll come back." As I try to soothe myself, a small voice inside my head shouts me down. "He lives twenty minutes from your house and knows the address and still he doesn't visit. Dad doesn't want you." I pound the pavements, stepping on every single crack I can. "I can stand on any crack because it doesn't make a difference. I used to think if I avoided them he'd come back to me. Anyway, I'm not listening to you any more." The voice comes back. "You can't ignore me because I am you."

The voice of doubt follows me all the way home and chases me upstairs and under my bed. I used to think that monsters lived under this bed and now I know monsters don't always hide. Sometimes they're in disguise, sometimes they live with you and pretend they care for you, only to change their mind at a later date. Charles Scallybones joins me there, curling his body around me like a giant Quavers crisp. His heartbeat falls into rhythm with mine and I think we drop into a damp, uneasy sleep, because the next thing I know a text jolts me and I bang my head on the underside of the bed.

Where r u? U disappeared from the hotel without saying where u were going. R u with a friend and 4got 2 say? Ring me. Mum. x

I switch off my mobile and bury my nose into Charles Scallybones's fur. His head bobs up and a sandpaper tongue swishes against my nose before he slips his head back down between his paws and lets out a soft groan.

"You wouldn't let me down." I ruffle his ears and he opens one eye then closes it again. "You've always been here for me."

The next time I check my phone I've got five voice messages. In the first, Mum has got that ranty outraged grown-up voice on. She says if I don't contact her I'll be in big trouble. By "big" she means "the size of the entire world".

Messages two and three are much of the same except she threatens to sell my guitar if I don't ring. In the background I hear Grace shout, "Do it!"

Message four and Mum's voice is softer and she says she loves me very much but I'm not allowed to run off like that. Mum says she's going home and she'll take the guitar with her. She expects me to phone her there.

In the fifth message Mum says that I'm all that matters to her. Grace shouts, "Don't I matter then?"

When I hear the key in the lock and Mum and Grace's voices in the hallway, I ease myself from under the bed. "Mum, I'm upstairs," I call weakly from the landing. I lean against the banister, waiting for Mum to shout so loud she blows my hair back, but she doesn't. Taking two stairs at a time, she runs towards me with her arms outstretched.

I'm enveloped in a cloud of vanilla cupcake scent. "Grace told me why you ran off and I'm so sorry you had to go through that."

Mum takes me by the hand and leads me back into my bedroom and closes the door. I bet Grace is downstairs moaning that I'm getting all the attention. Mum leans over and smoothes my hair and clucks about me being in wet clothing.

"What are dads for?" I bite my lip hard in an attempt to stop my eyes leaking. It doesn't work and a tear spills onto my cheek.

"Oh," Mum says, wiping it away with her sleeve. I can see a flash of worry in her eyes. Mum slips her fingers into mine. "I know you've had a rough ride with your dad but don't let that make you sad. A dad can be many different things to many people. Just because your dad felt he needed to move forwards in his life without us doesn't mean he's not still your dad. Do you understand? Is keeping him a secret the problem? I won't mind if you want to tell a close friend."

"I don't really want to tell anyone that Dad's on TV."

"I understand." Mum smiles, but there are tears in her eyes too. "We don't have to talk about Dad being famous. We could just talk about him being your dad."

"Do you believe in angels?" I ask, changing the subject.

Mum looks surprised. "There are many things in heaven and earth that I don't understand, and angels are among them. But if you want to believe in them that would be okay. There's no shame if it will help you."

"I don't believe in them. Jo in my class says they drop feathers to let you know everything is fine."

"Why are you asking me about this?" Mum looks at me. "I thought this was about your dad."

"Jo has her life sorted because she has something to believe in. That's the point. She believes things will always get better, in signs from above, in living happily ever after. She even believes in angels. I have nothing to believe in, not even a dad."

"I'm sorry, but I can't give you the answers."

"I'm waiting for Saint Gabriel to give me those."

"I'm confused. Where does Saint Gabriel fit into this?" Mum sighs but she's bewildered. Clearly, this conversation isn't going the way she had planned it.

"It doesn't matter," I say. "I just thought Dad was at the Amandine Hotel to see me in Project Eco Everywhere. I wanted him to watch me and be proud, but he ran away. So what? I won't lose any sleep over it." I shrug.

Mum shakes her head. "I know you and I know it

hurts so I want to let you in on a secret. You might have forgotten this but I want to remind you." She leans closer to me and I can smell vanilla batter rising from her neck. "Dad loves you."

The words make me take a sharp breath. I don't think I've heard her say that in the last four years.

"Dad loved you before and still loves you now, in his own way."

In his own way. That spoils it. I don't like the way Mum added that to the end of the sentence. It suggests his way is different to that of normal fathers out there. The truth is: I don't like Dad's way. I want to be the same as everyone else. I reach my hand under the bed and bring out the treasure chest holding Saint Gabriel and show the medal to Mum.

"Jo gave me this and said it would heal me but it hasn't. All it has given me are weird dreams about Dad."

"It's pretty," says Mum, looking at it and handing it back to me. "I don't know if a medal can heal you or give you the answers you're looking for, but angels and saints aside, you've got me." I inhale, ready to say something only Mum stops me. "And I know I can't be a mother *and* father to you, but I want your happiness more than anything in the world. I'm sorry your dad did what he did. I'm also sorry he stopped contact with you. Children think adults never do anything wrong, but they're human and sometimes they slip up and make mistakes. But despite all that, a long time ago, Dad gave me a wonderful gift."

"Was it a skateboard?"

Mum smiles and shakes her head. "The wonderful gift Dad gave me was you. I'm always going to love him for that." With that, Mum rises, kisses me on the top of my head, and makes her way to the door, before turning back. "You deserve happiness and I love you enough for two parents."

I smile as she slips out of my bedroom. When she's gone and can't hear me, I whisper, "I love you too, Mum – but you're right you can't be a mum *and* a dad."

CHAPTER 23

The envelope has my name on it, although I don't recognize the writing. Carefully, I pick it up from the mat and carry it upstairs to open alone. Why I do this, I don't know. It's not as if I'm expecting any post. I can't even remember the last time anyone wrote me an actual letter. Expectation travels down my spine as I slip my finger under the flap. As the envelope splits apart, it reveals a piece of carefully folded lined paper.

DAN, GET ON WITH YOUR LIFE. IT IS TIME

FOR YOU TO MOVE ON. FORGET ME. DAD.

The letter is written in capital letters, as if Dad is screaming at me. I turn it over to see if it says anything else on the back. It doesn't. I look at the envelope for more clues. There are none. Even Sherlock Holmes would soon realize this isn't much of a mystery. It's simply an angry note from a father who doesn't want his son. He knew I was at the Amandine Hotel and left straight away and then posted this letter to make sure I got the message. It is clear to me that Dad is dumping me once and for all. Operation Baskerville is over.

My dad is heartless. I *will* forget him. It's nothing less than he deserves.

From now on, I'm going to get on with my own life. And I'm going to help Mum get on with hers. She is broken-hearted without Big Dave and if she's sad, I'm sad. So Operation Reichenbach is... um...right 'n' back. Part of this is our fault, mine and Grace's. She set his house on fire and I helped her do it without even realizing. Together we've split Big Dave and Mum up over a stupid pink dressing gown. But I'm going to put everything right. If there is a glimmer of hope, no matter how small, that Mum and Big Dave are meant to be together, then I want to help them take it. (This time I'm going to believe Big Dave is innocent until proven guilty.)

Later that evening, I march up Big Dave's pathway full of bravado, but as I press the bell it ebbs away. What if Caroline 1973 answers? What will I say to her? She might cut me with her razor-sharp hair or set her zebra raincoat on me. This seemed like a brilliant idea when I was sitting in my bedroom and now I'm not so sure.

The door flies open before I can run away.

"Dan?"

"Christopher?"

"Dan?"

"What are you doing here?" I stare at him.

"I live here." Christopher stares at me.

"But Big D-D-Dave lives here," I stammer.

"Yeah, and he's my dad." Christopher blinks away his surprise. "Do you want to see him about a car repair?"

Big Dave appears in the hallway. "I don't think this is about a car, Kit. Dan, come in. I think we should talk."

I walk into the house, trying to process the fact that Big Dave just called Christopher – my *friend* Christopher – Kit. Wasn't Kit supposed to be Big Dave's five-year-old son? Wasn't he the child in that photo? None of it makes sense, but I follow them inside, where I can smell burned toast and burned curtains (probably courtesy of Grace).

"We were just making dinner," says Big Dave. "Do you want some?"

"Er, no," I reply. "It's Thursday. Microwave chips night."

"Oh right," says Big Dave, wiping his hands on his jeans, before moving a cardboard box and sitting on the sofa. "To be honest, we were only having beans on toast. But if you change your mind about joining us, we've got some burned toast with your name on it. Anyway, find a space and sit down. What can I do for you?"

Footsteps come down the hall towards the living room. *Caroline 1973* walks in and extends her hand. "It's lovely to meet one of Kit's friends." I recognize her from the kiss on the doorstep.

Christopher says, "Aunty Yvonne, this is Dan from my class at school."

"You're not *Caroline 1973*?" I mutter. "You're not Big Dave's wife?"

She clamps her hand to her mouth to stop herself from laughing. "I'm his sister. Who on earth is *Caroline 1973*?"

Big Dave looks down at his bicep and traces the tattoo with his finger. "I know. *Caroline 1973* is the name on my arm. It's my favourite song by Status

242

Quo and the year it was released. I got the tattoo years ago. Caroline wasn't my wife. Caz was. I've no idea who the real Caroline was. I think you'd have to ask Francis Rossi and Bob Young. They wrote the song."

"I've already told you my mum is called Catriona," says Christopher, "and I said she was somewhere in Scotland. Mum and Dad aren't together."

In the end I manage to splutter, "I think I've made a horrible mistake."

Big Dave turns his broad face to mine and tells me not to worry. But guilty thoughts are tiptoeing through my head. I allowed myself to get mixed up about all this because I don't trust people the way I used to. Look at what Dad did – I trusted him and he let me down. It was easy for Grace to persuade me that Big Dave would do the same. I let myself be convinced he was cheating on Mum. Instead, it's me who has let Big Dave down.

Christopher looks at his dad and asks if I'm his girlfriend's son. "Is this the new brother you mentioned?"

"It is," says Big Dave. "Kit, meet Dan. Dan, meet Kit."

Christopher bursts out laughing. "This is totally ridiculous and ace at the same time."

"You get Ninja Grace thrown in for free," I say,

"and remember my dog from tae kwon do? Well, you get to share him too."

"I wonder what he'll make of Boo?"

"I bet Boo makes him puke," I say. "Everything makes my dog sick."

"Would we be sharing a room if we move to your house?" Christopher looks at Big Dave, who looks at me. I nod, because even though there isn't enough room to swing a kitten it would be fun to share with Christopher.

"If Dan says it's okay, then it's okay," says Big Dave.

It turns out this whole thing was such a mess that it rivalled the supermassive black hole. For a start, Christopher never talked about his new school or his classmates to his dad. And he never wanted to discuss his dad's girlfriend and her family. "Every time I mentioned your mum, Kit went la-la-la and stuck his fingers in his ears," Big Dave tells me.

"I did not," replies Christopher.

"And I tried to bring him with me on a Tuesday evening for dinner."

"But I was at tae kwon do."

"It wasn't just about tae kwon do, you weren't ready to meet them and that's okay. Some things just can't be rushed," says Big Dave.

"Like gobstoppers," I reply, before adding, "but

you knew we were at the same school, right?"

Big Dave says that he did but he didn't put two and two together because there are three Year Six classes at Our Lady of the Portal and Kit never mentioned me. What's more, when Big Dave talked about Kit to me, I didn't seem to recognize the name. In the end, he simply thought we didn't know each other, but then he saw us at the Amandine Hotel together and it was obvious we were best mates. "By that stage your mum and me weren't getting on, so I slipped in and out again quietly," says Big Dave. "I thought everything was complicated enough."

To be honest, I'm not much of a Sherlock Holmes after all, because I didn't realize that Kit was another name for Christopher. And I didn't know Caz was short for Catriona.

"But now we know it was all a big misunderstanding, you'll come and live with us, right?" I say.

"I'm not sure," Big Dave says. "I thought you and Grace didn't want me in your house. After the fire incident and this whole business about the pink dressing gown..."

"Yes," replies Yvonne. "The dressing gown you're talking about is mine. I thought I'd lost it. I'd like it back, please."

Big Dave tells her that he doesn't mind buying

her another one, but I promise Yvonne she'll have her own dressing gown back *and* a bottle of Poison. She grins and says she can live without the perfume. This is a result, because I think it's probably very expensive and I've only got three pound coins and two tiddlywinks counters in my money box.

"Big Dave," I say, "I've got a bright idea…"

Who knew fairy lights had a life of their own? Christopher is trying to get them twisted and taped onto the living room wall, while I'm trying to get the second strand of fairy lights off the Christmas tree. Meanwhile, Grace is spraying the room with a musky body spray that is likely to suffocate us before Mum gets home.

The fairy lights fall onto Christopher's head and he swats them away and then tries to put them back onto the wallpaper with a wodge of sticky tape. "Do you think it'll work?"

Half the Christmas tree comes away as I untangle my set of lights. Baubles skitter across the floor and pine needles fall into soft pyramids. Charles Scallybones gives them a sniff, presumably wondering if they're dinner, but when I tell him "No", he moves onto chewing the tassels on Grace's handbag instead.

"We don't have long. An hour tops. Mum's shift at Aladdin's finishes soon," says Grace, giving the room another spritz.

I wind my fairy lights around Christopher's and tape them to the wall. "Come on, plug these lights in and let's see if they work."

Grace switches off the main lights and flicks on the fairy lights. "Incredible," she says, clapping her hands. "How romantic. I can't believe my little brother thought of this." She flicks all the lights off again and we stand in darkness.

When we hear the key turn in the lock, we all dive into the corner of the living room, except Big Dave, who is frankly too big to go anywhere. Christopher and I have our guitars and Grace has promised she will sing. Earlier, I offered her a pound and my tiddlywinks counters if she didn't sing, but she refused and said she has the voice of a mermaid. (I suppose she has a point, because when she opens her mouth it usually sounds like she's warbling underwater.) For a second, none of us speaks. In fact, the silence is as thick as Grace's make-up – until Mum sets down her bags and yells, "What the heck is going on here? It is pitch-black in this house. We can afford light bulbs, you know. And why does it smell like an explosion in a perfume factory?"

As Mum enters the living room, Grace hits the

switch on the fairy lights and the living room wall flashes with a twisted D and V inside a big heart. "Holy Mary, Mother of God," exclaims Mum, staring up at the flashing fairy lights taped to the wall.

I think we can safely say she's surprised.

Big Dave reaches out his arms and pulls Mum in for a hug and tells her how much he loves her and how he's here to stay. Meanwhile, Christopher and I start playing "Over the Rainbow" on our guitars. We know it doesn't exactly fit in with the Christmas theme, but then you can't have everything. Grace is attempting to sing and the dog has moved on to eating some stray pretzels that I accidentally tramped into the carpet yesterday.

"Are you trying to give me a heart attack?" asks Mum, pulling away from Big Dave. "What is all this in aid of?"

I set down my guitar. "Mum, you deserve happiness and Big Dave can give you that."

She raises an eyebrow and then grins. "Isn't that what I said to you, without the Big Dave bit?"

"Yes, and it's what I'm saying to you too." I walk over and stand between Mum and Big Dave. "You two are meant to be together because...um..."

"We love each other?" Mum smiles.

"Nope, because you're having Little Dave and he's going to need a dad. And you keep forgetting to make my lunch and I've got to share Jo's. I don't like eating green sludge."

"And you must be...?" Mum turns her attention to Christopher.

"Kit."

"I thought so. I'm so happy to meet you in the flesh, Kit. Ever since we spoke on the phone, I've wanted to meet you." Mum is glowing with such happiness that it's like she borrowed my golden ectoplasm.

Everything has worked out just how I planned (except for the bit when Charles Scallybones brings up pretzels on the sofa cushions and Mum tells us the baby is kicking and makes us feel her belly until she realizes it's just wind). Grace gives Big Dave back Yvonne's dressing gown and says she's sorry she thought it belonged to his wife. This in itself is a feat of gargantuan proportions, because Ninja Grace never says sorry for anything. Then Grace admits she quite likes Big Dave. Big Dave smiles and asks if she'd like him to teach her to drive. Suddenly she *loves* Big Dave.

Christopher and I leave Mum and Big Dave to talk about the future, which translates into discussing how to take the sticky tape off without ripping the wallpaper. We take Charles Scallybones for a walk through Paradise estate and down past The Frying

Squad, where two people are snogging in the alleyway. The boy looks up for a second before going back to kissing the chops off the girl. I swear I recognize him, but in the half-light of the alleyway I can't be sure.

"Walk a bit faster," urges Christopher. "Even the abominable snowman would freeze in this weather."

I tear my eyes away from the boy and catch up with Christopher and Charles Scallybones. When we take the turning onto the scrubby land, I tell Christopher I'm so happy he's my brother. "You can borrow my mum now."

"And you can borrow my dad," replies Christopher.

I think about it for a second before responding. "Thank you, but I've still got my own dad."

"Well," says Christopher, kicking up frozen clods of earth, "it's up to you. I'm happy to borrow your mum, because mine doesn't even write to me."

I feel like a fraud. My dad has written to me, but it's not a letter I'd want to show anyone. Although it still hurts, I read somewhere that if you let something go it will come back to you. So this is my new tactic in regard to Dad. Let him go and eventually he'll come back. Why didn't I think of it before?

We walk over the wastelands of Paradise, two boys about to start a new adventure and one dog eating discarded fast-food cartons.

CHAPTER 24

Ever since we did our guitar performance, school has been ace. I've signed a million autographs (okay, two) and one of those was on a plaster cast on the leg of a girl in Year Four. She said she wasn't really allowed to have it signed but when I was famous it would be worth something. (Only then she added the cast will be whipped off soon and she couldn't help it if I ended up in the hospital bin.) Christopher got asked for his autograph too and he did this amazing lightning flash instead of a dot over his "i". So I asked him if I could autograph his stomach and when he pulled up his shirt I drew my "a" around his belly button and then chuckled all the way to class. There's nothing like permanent marker to give you a laugh on a Monday morning.

Jo is our official groupie. When I tell Christopher Jo likes him now that he is a rock star and they could pair up, he tells me he's off girls – apparently they're too much like hard work. "Anyway, there's no way I could compete with saints even if I wanted to," he tells me, before running off to play football, weaving around a star-struck Jo, and firing the ball between the goalposts.

We've signed a deal with Kevin to be our agent/ bodyguard. We've said that if he lines up all our fans, we'll sign autographs for fifty pence. Kevin then gets ten pence commission per customer. Unfortunately, we only make one pound in the whole deal and Kevin takes his twenty pence commission and then takes the other eighty pence which he says is his retainer fee plus tax. As for his bodyguarding duties, well, they don't amount to much more than him chatting up any girls who head in our direction.

It's not just at school where things have changed. Big Dave, Christopher and Boo have moved into 10 Paradise Parade. Christopher and Boo are in my bedroom and Charles Scallybones is equally fascinated and horrified by the furry creature that keeps running around on a wheel but never gets anywhere. From time to time he thinks about eating Boo's food but ends up furious at not being able to get his teeth through the cage bars.

By Christmas Day we're one big happy family, plus Ninja Grace, who hasn't said a thing all morning. (Not that anyone is complaining.) Mum says we're going to have the best Christmas ever. At lunchtime she spreads the table with a white tablecloth and puts fake tea lights on top. We're not allowed to have real candles since Grace burned down Big Dave's bedroom. We're also not allowed to talk about it. It is referred to as the-incident-that-cannot-be-mentioned.

When Mum asks Grace to put out the cutlery, Grace says, "Yeessshh," and then Mum asks if Grace has sneaked some of the Christmas sherry. "No," Grace says, placing knives and forks on the table. "It wooks wotten." Mum stares at her and then shoves a spoon in a bowl of steaming sprouts. There are so many they could create enough wind to work the turbines in the fields beyond the Paradise estate. When Big Dave sits down, he says sprouts are the devil's food but he'll eat them and be damned.

"I wussed to fink they were fairwy cabbwages," says Grace.

Big Dave's jaw drops open, which isn't pleasant since there's clearly a squashed fairy cabbage on his tongue. Grace goes red and passes a bowl of roast potatoes in his direction. Big Dave says they're also the devil's food and it's his duty to eat them to protect us all from their dastardly deliciousness. He proceeds to pop one in his mouth. Steam bursts from his pursed lips and he has to quench his mouth with a whole can of beer, downed in one.

After lunch, Mum brings out the snowy-peaked Christmas cake. I make a mental note to encourage Mum to give Grace the piece with the reindeer on top.

In our house it's traditional to open our presents after dinner. What's not traditional is Grace opening her mouth to thank Mum for the perfume and Mum screaming, "Why, in God's name, is there a chunk of sprout still stuck to your tongue?" It isn't a sprout. It is a stud. Grace looks wounded (more wounded than having her tongue stabbed with a needle and a silver ball inserted). She says she got it done on Christmas Eve as a treat to herself. Mum says she needs a lie-down as a treat to *herself* and we'll have to open the rest of our presents without her.

Mum has bought me a new mobile phone and when Grace offers to put some more of her glittery stickers on it I offer to get a magnet and see what effect it has on metal tongue studs. That shuts her up. Well, that and the swollen tongue. Christopher gets a huge new hamster wheel, which is like the London Eye for rodents. Big Dave bought me a new book on Sherlock Holmes and a sky lantern set and tells me I can make my own super-duper deluxe version now. Grace gets an envelope from Big Dave and looks disappointed until she realizes there's a piece of paper inside offering her ten driving lessons. That's when I wonder if I should have given Big Dave an envelope offering him trauma counselling instead of a book on repairing cars for idiots. He thought it was hilarious – the book, that is – but it wasn't meant to be a joke. It was all I could find in the bookshop for the amount of money I had. Signing autographs doesn't pay much these days.

Grace spends the rest of Christmas Day picking food out from under her stud and I spend it wondering if Dad is, at this very moment, eating Christmas pudding with the beefy boy. I did break my promise not to bother with Dad by dropping a Christmas card through his letter box. It had a load of beans in Christmas hats on the front. It's the best Christmas there's ever bean, it said. I didn't write my name inside. I chickened out and tried to content myself with the fact that something I'd touched landed inside Dad's world, even if he didn't know it was from me. Dad didn't send one to me but then I didn't expect one – even though I sort of thought if

I let him go he'd come back. Incredible things *don't* happen, even if you're mates with Saint Gabriel.

That's another thing – I think about giving Jo her medal again, but something holds me back. I don't know if it's the Dad situation that's preventing me feeling truly happy. Everything else in my life is going well. It's just this one thing – one thing that can't be perfect. Jo hasn't asked me for the medal back either. She's moved on to making her own rosary beads from the tears of baby unicorns. Actually, I think she's making them from broken necklaces she bought at the charity shop but, whatever, she hasn't remembered I've got Saint Gabriel.

So Saint Gabriel has decided to live with me, where I think he's quite happy as a castaway on the pirate island. Charles Scallybones tried to eat him once but I managed to grasp him from the jaws of certain death. Instead Charles Scallybones ate

a monkey and a palm tree and I was happy that I saved Saint Gabriel's life. That means I could be a saint myself. Saint Daniel of Hope has a ring to it.

Another thing – I've stopped having those Dad dreams, the ones where I'm buried under leaves and Dad's hand reaches out. And I don't think I miss them.

CHAPTER 25

Quite where the past five months have gone I don't know. The infection in Grace's tongue has healed and she can now speak without lisping. Mum looks like she's swallowed a bowling ball and Big Dave and Christopher have moved in for ever. Things have been pretty good in the Hope household – in fact, they're better than I could have imagined. Big Dave has showed me how to take apart an engine, just like he promised, and Grace has had seven driving lessons and managed to scratch the paintwork on the Mondeo.

Dad is still on the telly but I don't watch him as

much as I used to. Seeing him all the time is like picking at a scab. I do it and it hurts for a while. When it heals, I pick at it again and go through the whole process over and over. The result is that I never heal. I made a New Year's resolution, even though I don't believe in them. I said to myself that I'd get on with my own life for at least eight whole months without obsessing about Dad. For a few months it worked, but today it feels as though a meteorite has landed on my head.

"Dan, there's something I'd like to mention," says Mum, rubbing Little Dave in her big belly. "I saw your dad."

My stomach skips as if it's a pebble skimming across a still lake. If they've met up, this must be big news. Mum never really talks about him and they've not had contact for years. It's obvious he wants to communicate with me again. *Skip, skip, skippety-skip*. This is what I've dreamed of. *Skip, skip, skippety-skip*. Everything's going to turn out all right. *Skip, skip, skippety-skip*.

"He's not looking too well. In fact, he looks poorly. I hardly recognized him."

Skip, skip, skippety-sink.

"I could have lied to you, but I think it's better if you know what I saw. Dad was there in the hospital when I went for my check-up. He didn't see me but

I saw him walking down a corridor." Mum takes the palm previously rubbing Little Dave and rubs my hand in circular motions. "I think he must be ill, judging by what I saw."

"But he's on the telly," I reply, pulling my hand away. "You can't be ill and on the telly." Mum is exaggerating things.

Putting on a brave face, I pretend I'm not bothered anyway, but a few hours later, when I'm taking Charles Scallybones out, it's all I can think of.

There are degrees of sickness. When Big Dave is sick on a Saturday morning, Mum calls this self-inflicted. A bacon-and-egg butty smothered in brown sauce usually sorts him out. Charles Scallybones is always sick, but the vet says he's very healthy for a dog with an entire pirate ship in his stomach. Ninja Grace is sick in the head, but nothing can help her. So where does Dad fit into this scale? Either way, it can't be too bad, because he's got a serious job. If he was as sick as Mum is hinting at, then he'd be in bed, not under the bright lights in a studio. But I feel uneasy. When I get a chance, I'm going to write Dad a proper letter. I'm going to put my heart into every word, just like Mrs Parfitt asked us to do when we were writing about our hero. I'm going to make it impossible for Dad to ignore. I'm going to hand-deliver it as well. Then I'm going to look Dad straight in the eye and tell him I need him.

The following evening, when I'm staring at a blank sheet of paper and figuring out what I can write to Dad, Mum starts huffing and puffing and wandering around the house, grabbing things and throwing them into a bag. "It's a bit early," she keeps muttering. "I must get myself sorted." She blows out softly. Out. In. Out. In. Little Dave rises and falls inside her belly.

"What's early?" I drop the piece of paper that reads, *Dear Dad*.

"There isn't time," pants Mum. "I need you to ring an ambulance. After that, I need you to find Big Dave. He's gone to see a customer and then he's going to his Kwik Kars workshop." Mum tries to smile but it's an effort. "The idiot has left his mobile phone in the kitchen."

"Grace could drive you to the hospital," I say, my voice rising.

"She left a note on the kitchen table. Read it. I think she says she's at Stan's house for dinner. Anyway, Big Dave has the car and I want to get to the hospital in one piece because..." Mum stops mid-sentence and concentrates on breathing like it's the hardest thing she's ever had to do. But breathing isn't all that difficult because I do it every day. "Never mind, just ring the ambulance."

I'm already dialling 999.

Hello, which emergency service do you require?

Ambulance, please, for 10 Paradise Parade.

It is on its way, but can you tell me a little about the patient?

Her name is Val Hope and she's average height with blonde hair. Oh, it's not really blonde. Does that matter? She gets it done in Crops and Bobbers, although she says what they charge for bleach is criminal. She won't eat chips from the chip shop and she wears this perfume that smells like cupcakes. I've forgotten what it's called.

Thank you, but I wanted you to tell me a bit about what's wrong with the patient.

Oh, why didn't you say?

I thought I had.

Mum is having a baby.

I see. What is she doing right now?

She's calling Big Dave – that's the dad – all the names she can think of. Some of them sound rude.

Have you counted the time between contractions?

What is a contraction? Is it like subtraction? I can't think straight because Mum is mooing.

Stay calm. Do not worry about the

262

contractions. The ambulance is nearly with you. And take care of...

Myself? I will.

I meant the patient.

When they arrive, the paramedics don't seem to want my hot towels. "Stick them in the washing machine," says one. "We're not in a TV drama," says the other, rolling Mum away in a wheelchair. Well, that's pretty obvious, because if we were in a TV drama they'd need the hot towels. That's where I got the idea in the first place.

Mum smiles weakly as they put her on this metal lift and, just before they hoist her into the back of the ambulance, I put something into her palm. "I  love you," she says, looking down at it. I definitely think I was supposed to say "I love you" back but I waited until the ambulance doors were closed and then it seemed a bit silly to give her an answer when she couldn't hear it.

The second the ambulance turns the corner I put on my coat and run down the street towards Big Dave's workshop. By the time I reach it I can barely breathe and there's a stitch in my side so big it could sew together a giant's trousers. It looks deserted but I try the door anyway. The workshop is locked. I stand in the middle of a patch of grass and nettles and wait for Big Dave. He can't be far away now, I tell myself. That customer won't keep him long. Any minute the Mondeo will swing around the corner and come down the alley towards me.

It doesn't.

CHAPTER 26

I spend ten minutes texting Grace and Christopher, who is at this moment in tae kwon do and probably kicking the living daylights out of the air. Then I spend the next ten minutes counting the number of dog poos there are in the alleyway. Five at last count, although I think there might have been six and I stood in one. As I'm wiping my foot on the nettles and getting my legs stung, a car swings into the lane and catches me in its headlights. I jump up and down, waving my arms.

"Dan?" Big Dave pokes his head out of the car window.

I explain Mum's in labour and jump into the car. It's fantastic. We're like two cops zooming down the road after the villains. The tyres squeal as Big Dave takes the corners at speed. All we need is a flashing blue light. When the traffic lights turn red, Big Dave bangs on the steering wheel and screams, "Hurry up! Pray for green all the way."

I do and I think it works on at least four sets of lights. The fifth set flash amber, but that's because my mind has wandered off to the folic acid I gave Mum. I don't know where the thought comes from or why I even remembered it, but I have.

"If Mum took two folic acid tablets is that the same as an overdose?"

"Huh?" Big Dave takes the corner so sharply I'm catapulted to the side of the car and bang my arm on the door. "Don't be ridiculous. She was supposed to take folic acid."

"I know," I reply, rubbing my arm, "but I think she accidentally got one extra by mistake."

"A stray folic acid tablet hardly counts as an overdose. I don't know where you get these strange ideas from but I want you to stop worrying. I'm only rushing to the hospital because I want to be there for the birth."

I settle back in my seat to check the spreading poppy-shaped bruise coming up on my arm.

Big Dave does make it in time. While he's in with Mum, I hang around the corridor with ten pounds to spend. Big Dave pulled a ten-pound note out of his wallet and didn't have time to take it back and give me change instead. You can buy a lot of chocolate with ten pounds. I've eaten five chocolate bars and started a packet of pickled onion crisps. It is a fact that chocolate and pickled onions don't go together.

When Grace joins me, I hand her what's left of the crisps and say, "It was you."

A crisp-crumb fountain sprays from Grace's mouth. "It was me what?"

"Months ago I got this letter from Dad. Only it wasn't from him. It was from you. You pretended to be Dad. And you would have got away with it if I hadn't just seen the note you left for Mum. You'd written it in capitals. You do a funny-shaped E, like a backwards 3, when you're in a hurry. I've never noticed it before."

Grace blushes and she looks down until her eyelashes tickle her cheeks. "You don't hate me, do you?" She doesn't even attempt to deny it. "I'm sorry. Dad hurt you so much at the Project Eco Everywhere show that I wanted you to forget him. I knew the only way was to make you think that he was asking you to get on with your life. If I'd told you to get on with your own life you wouldn't have listened."

"No," I say carefully. "I wouldn't."

Grace scrunches the crisp packet into a ball and stuffs it into her pocket. "I did it for you."

"You must miss him too."

She turns away. "I try not to think about it."

I feel a twist of regret when I realize that Grace only turned into a ninja when Dad left us. That's when she first got angry and mean. Not once did I think being without a dad would affect her that way. It's as if I've been in a car wash all this time and it's only now that the foam is clearing. Dad used to call her "Princess". No one has ever called her that since and I bet it hurts.

Grace's mascara is smudged and she looks like a scared panda and although I want to be angry I can't be. "It's okay," I say. "I'm not annoyed. You probably did me a favour. You're not a Ninja Grace, really. You're sort of Princess Grace." I almost choke on the words as I clutch her fingers. Half-bitten nails coated in glittery nail polish close around my hand and she smiles weakly. Then she pulls away and reaches into her coat pocket.

"I've wanted to give you this for ages. When I was looking for the walkie-talkies, I found a list under your bed. You can't keep things from your sister, you know. I realize you've been sad too and, even though you crossed it out, I got you this.' Grace pulls a small red toy rocket from her coat. On the side she has written HOPE 1 in white nail polish. "You don't really want a new sister, do you? I saw that on the list too."

"No," I reply, taking the rocket in one hand and squeezing her with my other. "I'm happy to stick with the one sister I have."

"You have more than one sister now." Big Dave appears in the reception area with a goofy grin on his face. And just as he's telling us that Mum has given birth, Christopher turns up in his white dobok, which, when you think about it, is pretty appropriate, because most people in the hospital look like they're wearing one too.

We hurry into a side room where Mum is sitting up in bed, and beside her is a basin holding pink blancmanges.

"Mum, you've got someone else's baby by mistake," says Grace, peering into the basin.

"No," Mum says. "They both belong to us. Surprise, surprise: twins."

Big Dave tells us they knew it was twins all along but didn't want to tell us. "We wanted to keep it as the biggest surprise ever. We thought you might spot it on the scan, but you didn't."

I look at baby number one, who is snuffling softly like a little piggy. "I thought the scan looked like a prawn," I say, adding, "I couldn't even see one baby."

"The second was hiding behind the first one." Mum claps her hands in delight. "This is the beginning of our lives together." She beckons me over and asks me to open my palm and then drops something back into it. "Here, this belongs to you. It made us happy today, because look what we've got." Mum points to the twins. "And they're both healthy and beautiful girls. That's three sisters now, Dan and Christopher. You're going to be outnumbered."

I stare down at the red rocket in one hand and Saint Gabriel in the other. I've had him over six months now, so surely I can give him back. Mum has had the babies and says we're all happy, so I don't think things could get any better. But, to be honest, I'm going to miss having Saint Gabriel. I'm not sure what help he's given me but, at this moment in time, the Hope family are content. Mum looks over and smiles at me and asks me if I want to hold a baby. I shake my head but she lifts one from the basin, instructs me to sit and plonks it into my lap. There isn't much I can do except look down at the blob and smile. It wriggles and I feel a rumble come from its bottom so I hand it back to our mum.

Mum smiles. "I think Big Dave's got a job there.

But while he's doing it, I wondered if you three could do a job for me? I'd like you to come up with names. Nothing too outrageous, mind. I don't want a Nectarine or a Harpoon or an Emmental."

Grace wants to call a baby Gracie, but I swear there's no way we're calling a baby after her. I think it would choke me. "What about Danielle? That's an epic name," I say.

"Or Christy," replies Christopher. "What about Kitty?"

It takes us ages to agree, but in the end we announce the names we've picked to Mum and Big Dave. "We'd like to call the babies Faith and Hope."

Mum looks shocked and then her face breaks into a huge grin. "They're the best names I've ever heard. They're absolutely perfect."

Not wishing to take all the credit, although they were my idea, I step forward and say, "I thought we should call one of them Hope as a way of connecting our two families. The baby will have our surname as its first name and then Big Dave's surname."

"Brilliant," says Big Dave. "You didn't consider Caroline? I've already got the name tattooed on me, so that would make it easy."

"Nope. We're sticking with Hope and Faith," says Grace, elbowing me out of the way, "because they go together."

Mum looks down lovingly at the babies and says, "With the twins, we are complete."

I set my red rocket in their basin and say, "Welcome to the world, Faith and Hope."

The following day, Faith and Hope come home and settle into drinking, sleeping, pooing and being sick. I think they've been taking tips from Charles Scallybones, who, incidentally, is quite stunned at having two new wiggly things in the living room. Not only that, he's eaten a bit of their muslin cloth and a tiny baby rattle. Still, it means I'll never lose him, because he rattles when he walks now.

I'm taking my role of big brother quite seriously. I've already explained how they can rival the supermassive black hole in my bedroom by creating one twice as big when they get older. Mum would relish this challenge. I've told them that skateboarding is the best fun you can have on four wheels, even better than a pram, and that mashed carrot is best when spat onto the ocean of swirly carpet.

I'm explaining how Grace needs to have her make-up and clothes borrowed at least once a week when I notice Dad's programme come onto the telly. I don't know why, but I stop everything and watch as a new woman reads the news, and when it comes to the weather she introduces a new weather girl. At first I think Dad has a day off, but then my stomach feels as though it's playing a game of Twister.

"And tonight," says the newsreader, gently tilting her head to the side, "we end on some very sad news." My breath catches inside my throat. "Malcolm Maynard, one of our own presenters, died in the early hours of this morning after a short illness. His career started when he was a journalist for a local newspaper and he worked his way up, eventually moving into television to much success. Malcolm Maynard is survived by his wife, Barbara Ann Maynard, and his son, Jeremy. Our condolences go out to the family."

The beefy boy is called Jeremy.

How can anyone be called Jeremy?

How can Dad be dead?

Jeremy?

Dad?

Dead?

The woman turns and faces another camera while saying, "That's it for tonight. We'll be back again tomorrow at six o'clock. Enjoy the rest of your evening."

With one catastrophic blow, the little Dad tree growing inside my soul is axed.

CHAPTER 27

I feel as though I'm about to jump off a huge diving board and into an endless ocean. I don't know how I'm going to land. I don't even know if I will survive the fall or if I'll drown when I get there.

I am weak; my legs boneless. "Dad, you can't go. Don't leave me yet. We're still going to meet. I am going to play 'Over the Rainbow' to you and you're going to be so proud of me."

A huge tidal wave of sorrow builds inside me: swelling, falling, rising once more and galloping in front of me like frightened foam horses. I stand on the board, my toes gripping the edge. Behind me is my old life. Sixty seconds ago I was a different person with two parents. I had hope that my dad would come back to me and scoop me up in his arms and beg for my forgiveness. And I'd give it, because I love him with all my heart. In front of me is an ocean. It means swimming for ever without Dad by my side. I don't want to jump into it, I don't. I want to go back down the ladder and stay where I am. But the ladder has crumbled and I have no choice but to dive forward into the future. And I want Dad to hold my hand through this but I know he can't.

I jump into the unknown, screaming.

The cushions are ripped and I watch, bleary-eyed, as fistfuls of white cloud stuffing fall through my fingers. I kick the coffee table and tear pages from the magazines and throw them high into the air. They flutter down on me like broken butterflies. And I howl, my heart heavy, and the sound of it is worse than any werewolf in any horror film. It comes from the darkness inside me and is so raw that Faith and Hope join with me in screaming. As Mum and Big Dave run into the living room to see what's going on, I force my way past them.

"Dad is dead," I holler.

I hear Mum gasp and she tries to hold me but I'm out of her grip and down the road before I hear her utter a single word. Ducking in and out of the traffic,

I weave through the estate and across the wasteground. Cars honk their horns. They can hit me for all I care. A train passes under the railway bridge and the force of it blows the skin on my face back. My feet carry me over the bridge and up Skateboarding Hill and, as I reach the top, the sun drops low in the sky. Birds scatter as I enter the twilight woods.

Dad has gone.

Thin sunlight seeps through the trees and shows dust in the air, like tiny Sea-Monkeys, bobbing around my trainers. Not far from where I'm slumped under a tree is Dad's house. *Was* Dad's house. Huge heaving sobs come from deep within and I bury my nose in my hands in an attempt to catch the tears, but they still manage to spill through my fingers and splatter onto my top.

How could Dad leave me like this?

The question hula-hoops round inside my head. I needed Dad to want me so much, I believed it could happen. I let the dream grow into a big tree. I don't even think I could see past it. I wipe my nose with my sleeve and run my finger along the trunk behind me. There was just one problem. My Dad tree didn't have roots. Without them, I'm left with nothing.

I lie broken, a cracked snail shell, underneath twisted branches and brambly bushes. Beyond the wood, the sun drops further in the sky, throwing long dark shadows over me like an uneasy blanket. I curl my body tighter and move my knees up so they are close enough to kiss. "What did I do wrong?" I whisper into the earth. "What did I do to make you ignore me? You've cheated me out of a dad. The one thing I wanted more than anything in the world. It was the last thing left on my Saint Gabriel list. Now I've got to score it off. It's your fault, Dad. Get back here and be my dad. Get back here and love me."

I need my dad.

After that there is nothing, only peace. Occasionally, a train steams through the town and I hear it sucking the air, but nothing more. Then I scream, "Help me understand!" and it's so loud that I can't believe it's come from inside me. Birds wheel into the sky, cawing and trying to escape the lunatic animal hiding in their woods.

Only when my lungs can't take any more pressure does the panic ease. I am quiet, deflated. I gather myself back up and ease my head against the tree.

"Dan!" I hear my name being called. Footsteps grow closer and I can hear huffing and puffing as someone heaves their large body up Skateboarding Hill.

"I'm here," I whisper, drained of energy. "I'm here." The words die on my lips.

"Thank goodness." Big Dave crouches down beside me and pulls me into a hug, which I don't pull out of. "We were so worried about you. I was worried about you. I thought you'd run away."

"There's nowhere to go."

"Even if there was, your place is with us." Big Dave lets me go from his embrace but maintains eye contact. "I'm sorry about your dad and I know nothing will make it better, but if you want to feel sad come and do it with us, rather than on your own. We're here for you, Dan. We're always here for you."

"I wanted a dad and now I've lost him and I can't ever get him back." My eye springs an unexpected leak and I have to quickly lick the tear away with my tongue and pretend it didn't happen. But I can't pretend, because another tear follows the first. And then another, until my face is streaked with rivers.

"I can't replace your dad," replies Big Dave, using his thumb to wipe away my tears. "But you can have me, son, if you want me."

Son.

Big Dave called me son.

Soft winds whisper through the trees, making green leaves fall and dust the tops of our heads. As Big Dave stands up and reaches out his hand, a sliver of low sunlight catches the hairs on his arm. I stretch my fingers towards his. We connect and his touch pulls me in. When I couldn't see the face in my dream, I always assumed the hand belonged to Dad...but it didn't. Big Dave turns his face to me and smiles.

Mum is waiting at the front door with Faith in one arm and Hope in the other. I pull free from Big Dave and run towards her, throwing myself into a four-way hug. She stoops down and tells me she's sorry about Dad. If I want to talk, Mum says she'll always be here to listen.

"It was a shock. I wanted Dad to speak to me so much and now he never will."

"I understand." Mum ushers me into the house and pops Faith and Hope into their baskets. "I've told you before that he loved you and I still stand by that. Perhaps he didn't love you in the way you wanted him to, but that doesn't mean there wasn't love there. I watched him hold you and I saw the love in his eyes."

"Can you switch off love?" I search Mum's face for the truth.

"I don't believe you can. Not truly. Not completely."

Big Dave slopes away but I tell him to stop. "Don't go. You're part of the family too." Big Dave halts and comes over and sits down. "Mum," I say, turning back to face her, "once upon a time, when I was sitting on the stairs, Dad whispered goodbye to me. But I didn't get to say goodbye to Dad and I want to, so badly."

"I'm not sure we can go to the funeral. I think it might be awkward with his new family there. Perhaps we can think of another way to say goodbye. We could plant something to remember him."

I bite my lip. "No, I think I've had enough of Dad trees."

"If you don't want to plant something then we could go to a beach and write his name in the sand or you could name a star after him."

"Thanks, but I don't want to remember Dad as a star either."

Big Dave eases himself out of the chair and disappears upstairs. I can hear him rummaging about in my bedroom and Charles Scallybones's barks as something falls. A bedroom door slams and Big Dave's feet thunder back down the stairs.

"This", says Big Dave, "is the perfect way to say goodbye." He hands me the box and I nod.

I know exactly what he's saying.

CHAPTER 28

Dear Dad,
Can I still call you Dad? It feels a little bit strange to say it, but it would feel even weirder to call you Malcolm. So Dad it is. Mum says you'll always be my dad and that's all that matters. We're linked by blood, Mum says. Nothing can change this fact. I can't get rid of my blood, unless I get a visit from a vampire. Not even death, which you know more about than me, can stop us being father and son. Mum is right. She usually is, but I don't tell her.

I also know you have another son called Jeremy. Mum told me that he is Busty Babs's son from a previous marriage. I'm not jealous that he was your son too. I envied him once. But now I realize that I was lucky because I had you for seven years. He only got you for four and I think that's sad.

I still have the teddy bear you bought me when we got separated. Mum had to restuff him a few years ago because I'd squeezed him so hard his tummy exploded. His paws are blotchy where my tears have dripped onto them. This is all I've got left of you. I will treasure him. I just wanted to let you know this because it is important.

Another thing that is important to me is trying to understand what went wrong. I have a question and I'm just going to fire it out there into the universe in the hope that you can hear me. Did you love me right up to the end? Mum says you did. I want to believe her but I can't be certain. How will I ever be certain?

For now, I've decided to believe that you wrote me a birthday card every year of my life but you couldn't post them because you felt guilty. Somewhere in the world there is a small pile of birthday cards with my name on them.

Maybe in, like, fifty years, someone will find them and post them and a whole load of envelopes will drop onto my mat. Did you know that happens sometimes? I've read about postcards turning up at their destination fifty years after they were written. And even if I'm ancient and bald, they'll mean the world to me.

I feel sad so I've tried to turn this tear splash into a monster. I think it's quite a good drawing. I got a gold star in art recently.

Dad, I don't think you're a bad person. You can't be. Saying you're bad would be like saying I'm bad too. I'm part of you, after all. I'm going to make a list now, because it's not easy writing on ricepaper and my wrist hurts. I wish I had typed this but then that wouldn't have worked. Ignore me. Here is the list:

THE BIG LIST OF SAD THINGS

You didn't tell me you were dying. I wish you had. I wanted to say goodbye. This is the thing that hurts the most. When I pretend to die, I call everyone into the bedroom and do that raspy voice thing and then I take my opportunity to tell them how much I like or dislike them according to how much they've annoyed me at my chosen time of death.

Saying you love someone is very important. You should have told me, at least once. I'm always going to tell everyone I love them, except Grace. She knows I like her anyway because I take care of her. I told her about the time, months ago, when I saw Stan in the alleyway at The Frying Squad with his tongue in a strange girl's throat. It took me a while to realize it was him but in the end it was the fluff on his upper lip that gave him away. Grace was very happy with me for telling her and said having a brother to keep a lookout for her wasn't such a bad thing after all. And she gave me two pounds for my trouble, which I spent on bottom cream for Faith and Hope (more of them later). It was the only thing I could afford in the shop and I reckoned it was the gift that keeps giving. So, you see, I'm all about saying I love people in my own way.

You made a new life with new people and that's okay, but you can't forget the old people. Not that we're old people, but you know what I'm saying. We were still here, Dad. We were waiting for you to return. At least, I was. This makes me sad.

THE BIGGER LIST OF HAPPY THINGS

Mum is happy. Mum has Big Dave. They're going to get married in the autumn. I think you'd like him. I like him. He runs Kwik Kars and he can strip an engine in minutes, even if he can't spell Quick Cars properly. Big Dave used to be married to a woman called Catriona. I thought her name was Caroline, but that's a long story. I won't bore you with it now because I'm sure you're busy up there. Can you see the planets from heaven? Big Dave bought me a planet mobile once but Charles Scallybones ate it.

The guitar: that's one of my happy things. I'm awesome at the guitar. My best piece is "Over the Rainbow". I wanted to play it for you at our Project Eco Everywhere show but you left before you heard me. If you close your eyes now you can imagine me playing. Mum bought me a present recently. She said it was a gift from you. I didn't understand her at first. Turned out it was this silver guitar pick and she'd had it engraved. DAD IS "OVER THE RAINBOW" it said. Every time I play my guitar I let the music

285

travel on the breeze and perhaps it will travel to you. And every time I see a rainbow I will know you're just behind it, like an indigo-coloured zombie. Just out of my reach. I've started learning a new tune now. It's called "Caroline". I think you'd like that one too. Big Dave bought me the music. I've also joined a boy band. Mainly it's me and Christopher (more about him later too), and we're going to call ourselves The Papercuts, because I got one when I was writing down lots of ideas for band names. Who knew that paper was lethal?

Ninja Grace has taken up kickboxing. But that's okay, because I'm going to tae kwon do now. She dumped Stan for cheating on her and has a new boyfriend called Todd, Love God. Those are her words, not mine. Todd is okay and does not have a hairy upper lip or another girl attached to it. (Note: I tried to call her Princess Grace, like you used to, but then she nearly broke my arm because my dog ate her best ballet pumps and I thought this wasn't princessy behaviour.)

Christopher is my new stepbrother. Yes, me with a brother. I know it's bonkers but there you go. He's Big Dave's son and he's the same age as me. We're even in the same class at school.

We have history and fell out over a girl but it's all settled down now and we're best mates. Christopher was the person who introduced me to tae kwon do and I really love it. Christopher also plays guitar like me, only he's not as awesome. Grace says it doesn't matter that he's not such a great guitar player because he's much better-looking and that's what counts in a band. Ninja Grace must've been kicked in the head at kickboxing, because she makes no sense.

I have twin sisters. They're called Faith and Hope. They're living, breathing poo machines. I don't know what Mum is feeding them, other than milk, but what is coming out in their nappies smells like the foulest rubbish dump. Think rotten eggs on cabbage leaves on stilton cheese on cauliflower and you're halfway there. However, they're also a bit cute, for girls.

School is going well and I've got a good bunch of mates. I'm still friends with Jo Bister, by the way. She is completely obsessed with religious stuff now. A while back she gave me this medal of Saint Gabriel of Our Lady of Sorrows and told me to write a list of ten things I wanted more than anything in the world. Jo told me that, with the help of Saint Gabriel, one dream would come true. One dream would heal me and lift me from my sorrow. I kept the medal for months and one by one the things I thought I wanted fell from the list until I was left with this final thing. Number ten. At first, I thought I'd lost this dream but then I realized I hadn't. Recently I gave the medal back to Jo and she accepted it. To be honest, I'm not sure if Saint Gabriel healed me or I healed myself. All I know is that I spent a long time thinking my family wasn't perfect and then I discovered that it didn't matter, because it was perfect for me.

I'm happy.

That is all.

Your loving son,

Dan. X

We walk in silence, me lost in thought and Big Dave staring into an ocean of sky. Moonlight bathes us in silver water and the night air has a bite to it. Although my fingers are frozen, I try not to disturb what is in my hands. I carry it as though it's priceless: a tissue treasure cupped inside my fingers. The words bleed across the ricepaper and they blur as I try to hold back my tears. In my pocket are the matches Big Dave took from the kitchen cupboard and a photograph of Dad that I cut from the newspaper.

Big Dave comes to a stop and lays his hand on my shoulder and squeezes. He promises he'll be waiting for me when I'm ready to return. I nod and then carry on alone. Above me the sky is studded with diamond chips. The wind gently whips up and ruffles my hair and I know. I just know. I stop. It is time.

This is the moment I'm going to let go.

I've built myself up. Prepared myself for what I know I've got to do. I'm not saying it's going to be easy, because the bubble mountains rising inside my stomach tell me otherwise. I pull Dad's photograph from my pocket. A final kiss is delivered. The paper smells inky but I imagine the scent of Dad's spiced apple aftershave as I close my eyes. When I open them again, it's just me and Dad in a universe surrounded by a million stars.

"This is goodbye," I whisper, placing his photograph inside the sky lantern. "This is where I set you free and in turn you set me free."

My fingers shake as I light the candle and I hold the sky lantern in my hands for the longest time, afraid of letting Dad go. The candle burns so low I have to take it out and replace it with another. Again, I light the candle and the sky lantern tugs in my hands. It's as though Dad is desperate to be released and as the lantern pulls and twists I let it go.

Let Dad go.

The sky lantern rises softly into the night sky, starting out on its journey. I watch it, blinking back tears, and it's all I can do to say, "Goodbye, Dad. I love you," because my throat has closed over. A golden dot now, it bobs on the currents of air, higher and higher; far from my touch. And then it's carried high into the clouds beyond the Paradise estate. I don't see the light go out; it simply floats away over the horizon.

Gone from my view for ever.

A tear rolls down my cheek, knowing that this is my final goodbye to Dad. Yes, he said goodbye to me on the stairs when I was seven, but now I've had the chance to say mine. Not that it means I'll forget him. I won't. Not ever. Dad will always be a little jigsaw piece in my life. Perhaps not as big a piece as he was before, but if I removed Dad completely, the jigsaw wouldn't be right. So Dad's always going to be with me and no one can ever take that away. Despite the ache in my heart, I know everything is going to be okay. That's how I feel as the breath of a soft wind dries my tears. And that's how I feel as I turn to look at the trees behind me. They've come through the winter and now they're growing stronger and I'm going to do the same.

As I stride through the grass, I realize that this is a whole new beginning of Dan Hope. Far in the distance I can see Big Dave and when he spots me he waves. And that's when something really amazing happens. Something that makes me certain that it was okay to let Dad go, because he always loved me, no matter how much I doubted it.

A white feather.

Falls from nowhere.

Softly spiralling.

A white feather.

Like a solitary snowflake.

A white feather.

In an empty night sky.

A white feather.

Floats on the breeze.

A white feather.

An angel's calling card.

OPERATION HOPE:

Tell us what YOU thought of the book,
and start spreading the HOPE!

If YOU want to take part,
log on to
WWW.aboycalledhope.co.uk

hope

courage

laughter

heartache

love

ABoyCalledHope

Find out more about the world of

DAN HOPE

Brilliant downloads and fantastic competitions

Exclusive sneak peeks and extracts

News, reviews and interviews

Find out more about Lara

Galleries, doodles and pictures

www.aboycalledhope.co.uk

Why not tell your friends about

A BOY CALLED HOPE

Cut out the slip below, and spread the hope to the moon and back!

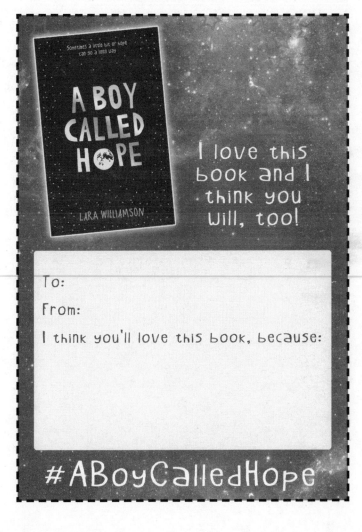

Sometimes a little bit of hope can go a long way

A BOY CALLED HOPE

LARA WILLIAMSON

I love this book and I think you will, too!

To:

From:

I think you'll love this book, because:

#ABoyCalledHope

A Girl Called Lara...

Lara was born and studied in Northern Ireland, graduating with a BA (Hons) in Fashion Design, before moving to London. After freelancing for various magazines including *Elle* and *More*, Lara settled at *J-17* as Beauty Editor, where she won a Jasmine Award for Best Article in a Youth Title.

After receiving an Honorary Mention in the SCBWI Undiscovered Voices 2012, Lara began writing *A Boy Called Hope* – her debut novel. She currently lives in London with her husband and daughter and likes daydreaming, tap-dancing and writing. Not at the same time.

Follow Lara on Twitter @LaraWilliamson

A Message from Lara...

This is the story of Dan Hope and me because without one there couldn't be the other. Growing up I had lots of big hopes and dreams. One that came true was writing for magazines. It took many years and a lot of hoping and dreaming before I started work at *J-17*. But in all that time I never gave up on the dream. Without knowing what it felt like to have those hopes and dreams I couldn't have written about Dan, the small kid with big hope in his heart. We share a lot in common. Dan would probably spell out **NO WAY** in potato alphabet shapes. But we do. And if I could write him a message on a sky lantern I'd say I can't walk like a baboon, I can't skateboard and I can't play "Over the Rainbow" on a guitar but I know what it feels like to have hope. Of course, life is no picnic sometimes, so I would also write and say Dan might see a lot of darkness before he can find the stars. Maybe I'd say he needs to feel the rain before he can see the rainbow. Finally, I'd say that no matter what life throws at him, a little bit of hope goes a long way. And then, just then, the sky lantern would fly.

Don't miss the next
novel from

LARA WILLIAMSON

The Boy Who Sailed the
Ocean on an Armchair

Coming 2015

Acknowledgements

In the words of Dan, I'd like to say a S-U-P-E-R-M-A-S-S-I-V-E thank you to all those who have supported and helped me complete *A Boy Called Hope*. Without your love, generosity and enthusiasm all hope would have been lost.

Huge thanks to my incredibly supportive and lovely agent, Madeleine Milburn. If I had some potato alphabet shapes I'd spell out ACE because that's what you are. Fact!

A special thanks to my amazing editor, Rebecca Hill, whose insightful edits and unfailing belief made Dan's hopes and dreams come alive on every page of this book. In doing so you made my own dreams come true. I cannot thank you enough.

If I could, I'd send a red rocket (with BIG THANKS painted on the side in white nail polish) to the entire team at planet Usborne who have worked so tirelessly behind the scenes to make this book what it is. And a special mention goes to Team Hope: Becky, Sarah S, Sarah A, Anna and Amy – I couldn't have done it without you.

Shelley Instone: you saw the heart in this story and you made it beat stronger. Thank you from the bottom of my own heart.

Thanks also to my cheerleading friends, Melissa Roske and Cat Clarke. You helped with plot, you read the story, you answered my questions – daft though they were – you helped me with titles and, most of all, were always there at the other end of the email when I needed you.

Sharon Healy and Jill Vosper: for all those Thursday tap evenings when you gave me your support. If I could, I'd do wings to celebrate this book but I am too afraid of breaking my ankles.

Huge hugs to all my Twitter friends, readers, bloggers and booksellers. I wish I could name you all but if you've tweeted, retweeted, read, blogged, recommended or sold on my behalf you have a special kicky-flicky foot snap of thanks from me.

Thank you to my mum and the Smyth family: David, Josie, Geraldine, Dessie, Peter, Joe and Ally (not forgetting Ben the dog). If ever I was searching for Paradise I found it with you.

Thanks as big as Jupiter to Thomas Howard, not only for reading the book but for putting on a deerstalker without complaint and to Matthew Howard for bringing Dan to life by being the best actor I could have wished for. You are both out of this world!

Heroes get a special mention in this book – Graham, you are mine. I could write a whole page on you alone because I owe you so much. And the last thank you goes to Millie. Without you Charles Scallybones wouldn't have had such a fabulous name. Without you I wouldn't have written a single word of this story. Without you there wouldn't be hope. This is your book, Millie, with all my love.

For more brilliant, funny and heart-warming stories, go to
www.usborne.co.uk/fiction